santino the eternal

By Sam JD Hunt

Edited by Missy Borucki & Kelly Mallett

Cover Design by Clarise Tan/CT Cover Creations

Cover Image by Eric David Battershell Photography

Cover Model Johnny Kane

Back Cover Images © Deposit Photo

MY BOUNTY IS AS BOUNDLESS AS THE SEA, MY LOVE AS DEEP; THE MORE I GIVE TO THEE THE MORE I HAVE, FOR BOTH ARE INFINITE. – WILLIAM SHAKESPEARE

"BE FREE, MY DARLING," he said to the languid corpse.

With the back of his hand, he wiped away the last drops of the precious nectar he'd drained from her fragile veins. "You have served me well." He watched as the ghost of his young victim fled her empty body.

He felt crushing remorse that he'd killed her. *Her death was kind, painless, and he needed her blood,* he convinced himself as he glanced around the darkened hotel room. The warm fluid rushing through him caused the sensation of a post-orgasmic high—so similar was the feeling that he craved the cigarette he usually only smoked after sex.

"No, not here," he said aloud to himself, his agile fingers placing the pack of cigarettes back into his designer suit coat.

The door to the hotel room opened—a swath of light from the hallway burned into his eyes and his hand instinctively reached up to shield himself from it.

A young housekeeper burst in, her eyes only glimpsing his form for seconds as he moved from the room with such preternatural swiftness that he was just a mere blur to her mortal eyes.

It was several more minutes before his perfected ears heard her scream in terror.

One

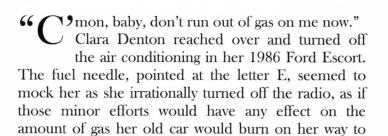

"C'mon, baby, don't run out of gas on me now."
Clara Denton reached over and turned off
the air conditioning in her 1986 Ford Escort.
The fuel needle, pointed at the letter E, seemed to
mock her as she irrationally turned off the radio, as if
those minor efforts would have any effect on the
amount of gas her old car would burn on her way to
work.

"One more mile," she said aloud to the
vehicle. "One more mile and I promise to feed you
after work. I can't be late again."

In her worn Fossil hobo purse her last ten
dollars sat crumpled. Clara hoped it would provide
enough fuel to get her back and forth to school that
week as well as to her job cleaning rooms at the newest
and classiest hotel on the Las Vegas Strip—the Roman.

Her stomach growled as she flashed her employee badge and pulled into the dark parking structure at the rear of the sprawling resort hotel and casino. At the place she'd worked before the employee facilities, those parts the guests didn't see, were austere. Here, however, even the employee parking garage was glamorous.

As she fled the car, terrified of punching in late again, she thought about how she'd never once seen the reclusive owner of the Roman—his name was Marchetti, she couldn't recall if she knew his first name. She assumed he was Italian, and rumors floated around that he was handsome, in his thirties, but even though he lived in the sprawling penthouse suite, no one she knew had ever seen him.

Clara's first three rooms were easy cleans, and in the second one she was able to nibble on an unopened bag of potato chips—she hadn't eaten since the night before when her roommate, Landon Miller, brought home scavenged baked ziti from the pizzeria he waited tables at.

The fourth room of her shift, however, was the one that changed the course of her life forever. As she flipped on the lights and walked in with her cleaning basket—maids at the upscale Roman weren't allowed to push carts into the rooms—she saw it. A foot poking out from the crisp white sheet of the king-sized bed. "Oh, sorry ma'am, I thought the room was..." She felt a rush of cool air blast past her, maybe even the faint hint of smoke, and then she saw it.

The foot protruding from the Italian 800 thread count Frette linens was not an alive foot. It was ghastly white; the red painted toenails a grotesque contrast to the paleness of the skin. *A prank,* she thought as she approached it, waiting for something to jump out at her. The air in the room changed, became oddly stagnant, as she sheepishly tugged at the sheet. Clara heard herself scream, as if a bystander, as her body crumpled to the floor.

"The police," she finally managed to mutter, as she reached for the phone on the mahogany desk. She stared at the phone, unable to remember how to get an outside line for several moments before deciding instead to press the button that was labeled *Emergency.*

Within minutes, several large men in dark suits blew into the room. One lifted her to her feet and asked if she was okay. As she nodded, he glanced at her nametag and said, "You may have the afternoon off, Clara. Thank you." He turned to look at the body as the other men donned latex gloves.

"Uh, we should call the police. This is the serial killer. It's got to be another of his victims—you know, the Blood Lust Killer."

The dark suited man in charge flung his body toward hers, his hands braced on his hips. "I believe it's time for you to go."

"No. You can't touch anything until Metro comes," she argued, her voice fighting to sound strong. *These men are tampering with a crime scene,* she thought. Her roommate, Landon, when not serving greasy pizza and pints of beer, was in the police academy. Clara had helped him study enough to know these men were breaking the law.

"Steven, please escort the former employee from the premises." He turned to face her once more, and with a sneer said, "We'll mail your final paycheck. Your services here at the Roman are no longer required."

She stood in shock, unable to process the dramatic turn that afternoon had taken. "You're firing me?" she finally choked out through her tears. The man never answered her, and she followed him to the central housekeeping department to return her uniform. The dark-suited stoic presence stood outside the changing room and walked her to her car, reminding her that security cameras would watch her exit the grounds of the casino.

In her hot car, with guards staring at her, she reached for her cell phone. Despite the glare of the suited Steven approaching her, she dialed 911 and switched it to speaker as she sped down the exit ramp. "Yes, at the Roman," she clarified to the dispatcher. "Room 80231—she was bloodless! White as a ghost." She paused as the dispatcher read back the information, then as Clara began to ask about the serial killer her phone went dead. *Damnit! Out of minutes!*

Moments later, she was fighting her way through traffic. "That jerk-off, how dare he fire me," she hissed into her empty car as she battled the throng of cabs down the small section of Las Vegas Boulevard that was known as the Strip. In shock, fuming and terrified, she barely remembered to make her left on

Flamingo when her car started to sputter. "Not the transmission again," she groaned before her eyes set on the fuel gauge. "Shit!" She covered her mouth with her hand—Clara rarely swore, and when she did, she shocked even herself. "I forgot to get gas!"

* * * * *

Flamingo was his least favorite place to drive. Stop after stop, he could rarely pick up the kind of speed he craved. When finally he was able to swoop around yet another annoying billboard truck, his designer-shod foot mashed the accelerator down as hard as he could. The Maserati lurched, pressing him back into the buttery leather seats that had been custom made to fit his tall, lean body. And then he nearly ran over her.

She fell backward into her battered old car, smashing into the dented frame and falling face down onto the dirty black pavement of Flamingo Road. "Fuck," he howled, the nimble car coming to a screeching stop as those behind him blew their horns and struggled to maneuver around him. He was able to stop his car at the side of the busy road, in front of the small frame of a young woman lying in the street.

"I didn't hit you, Miss, did I?" He sprang from his car toward her. *She's moving, that's good,* he thought as she placed her palms on the pavement, pushing her lean frame up.

"Um, no, I just, I thought you were going to hit me, I jumped and tripped."

"That is a relief." He reached for her hand and helped her to her feet, and as their skin touched, the electric shock between them went off like a hand buzzer.

"I-I'm fine now," she said with a quick tug of her hand to remove it from his. But he couldn't let go. He held onto her hand as a sensation so foreign, so *odd*, washed over him. *It was just a dry air phenomenon,* he convinced himself. *It wasn't the spark; it couldn't be, not with this simple girl.*

"Well, thank you for even stopping," she said with a smile, tugging her hand from his once more. This time he let her soft hand fall from his, but he continued to look into her eyes. They were brown, *chocolate brown,* he thought. She was young, twenty-one was the number that popped into his head as he stared at her mutely.

She ran her hand through her hair as she turned to face her car. "Do you need me to call a car service for you?" he asked as she lifted the rear hatch and pulled out a red gas can. "No, thank you, I'm out of gas. It's only a few blocks to the station."

"I would never let you do that. Please, I'll drive you."

She stared at the car—clearly he was a rich businessman, a local, and, she had to admit, breathtakingly handsome. But still, she was no idiot. She wasn't going to get into his car, or any stranger's car, with a blood-sucking serial killer roaming Las Vegas murdering young women. "I'm fine, I'll walk." She took a few steps and heard him speak again.

"No, Miss, you will *not.* I cannot let you do that."

"*Let* me?" She spun around and glared at him, empowered by the safety of the heavy traffic swirling around them like angry hornets.

He held up his hands in apology. "I didn't mean it like that, I'm sorry. What I meant was it would be ungentlemanly of me. I can call road service, or perhaps go retrieve your gas for you while you wait in the air conditioning of my car?"

"I'm sorry to snap. I've had a terrible day. I was fired from my job and, well, it's just been a rough one. I'd rather walk than wait, but thank you." She set off again, with the man only steps behind her.

He caught up to her, his suit coat removed and tossed over one arm in the oppressive heat of summer in Las Vegas. "My name is Santino, by the way, and it is a pleasure to meet you, despite the circumstances of our introduction," he said, positioning himself between the heavy street traffic and the young woman. "Miss...?"

"Clara Denton," she answered with a smile. *This drop-dead gorgeous rich guy is also a gentleman,* she thought as he reached to carry the gas can.

At the gas station, his phone buzzed. With a quick glance at it, he looked to Clara. "I'm sorry, I have to take this. I apologize for my rudeness." She nodded as he walked to the side of the gas station.

"Wait until I tell Landon about this guy," she said under her breath as she walked into the building to prepay for the gas.

Walking out, can in hand, the man, Santino, had his back to her. He was talking into his phone. She could hear him as she walked by toward the pumps. "Yes, Don, you did the right thing to have it cleaned. A mess like *that* in my home I would never tolerate."

Too bad he's a neat freak, she thought as she pumped the gas into the can, *not that it matters.*

* * * * *

An hour later, Clara was back in her apartment digging through her empty refrigerator. "No one ever buys milk," she said to the empty apartment. The foil pan of leftovers was the only palatable food she could find, so she finished it off while working on her paper for class the next morning. Her third year at UNLV was going well academically—she was a top student in the English Department, but financially she was in trouble. Student loans were piling up, and her passion was literature rather than a career field that would result in a lucrative job. Even if she taught, she knew her living conditions would be austere at best for the next decade.

As she looked at the research she'd done on a Word document on her MacBook, a spoonful of greasy baked ziti perched at her lips, there was a knocking at the thin door. "Landon, take your key once in a while," she shouted toward the door.

But Landon was not at the door. As she opened it, four members of the Las Vegas Metropolitan Police Department, or Metro as it was referred to locally, stood there. "Oh come on in," she said. *The police are finally here about the dead body,* she thought.

"We had a report of a crime from a resident at this address—a Clara Denton. Is that you?"

She nodded in relief. "Yeah, that's me. Is she related to the serial murders?"

"She?" The suited detective looked at his notes before making eye contact with Clara again. They followed her inside.

"The woman—the dead body I found at work today."

"Miss Denton, there was no body at the Roman. Not at the room number you reported, or any other room. Have you been following news coverage of the killings?"

"Well yes, but—wait a minute, there was a body, drained looking, white. The head of security and a few other men saw it, too."

"Miss Denton, I understand the stress you've been under. However, calling 911 with a made-up story is a serious crime. If we chased every baseless tip we'd be—"

"Baseless? I saw her!"

"You were fired today, were you not?"

"Well, yeah, because I insisted they call the police."

"According to management at the casino, you were fired for being late too many times. As you were leaving the resort premises, you called 911 from your prepaid cellphone and made up a story about finding a body in order to inconvenience the hotel."

Clara shook her head, the blood draining from her face. *Was this really happening?*

* * * * *

Santino paced on the priceless rug that graced the polished marble floors of his penthouse suite high atop the Roman. His trusted head of security, Donovan Salerno, sat on the cognac leather wingback chair and glanced over the notes in his small notebook. The afternoon had been stressful, but Don thought he'd done well.

"And the maid? She won't talk? Let's make her happy," Santino said as he rubbed his stubbly chin.

"Well, sir, we fired her, it was necessary that—"

"What the fuck did you just say? You *fired* her?"

Donovan took a deep breath and willed himself to stay calm. The boss was mad—deadly mad. He stood up and explained. "She demanded we call the police. That one, she was too smart. That young chick wasn't like the Mexican maids that most—"

"I swear to God, if you say one ignorant bigoted thing you will regret it for the rest of your short life." Santino had no tolerance for small-mindedness.

"Um, no, it's just this housekeeper was not going to be deterred from alerting Metro to the mess in your house, sir."

"So now she's out there, with no loyalty whatsoever to us, no incentive to stay silent. *That* is a problem, Don."

"Yes, sir. We'll take care of her. I apologize for letting her go."

"I don't want her *harmed*, I merely want her *silent*. What is her name?"

Santino's pale eyes focused on the man as he stopped his pacing. The words his head of security spoke caused him to grow cold, colder than his usual soulless body.

"Clara Denton."

* * * * *

Miles away, Clara sat in a chair, an angry Metro police officer staring at her as if she were the criminal. "Listen, I saw what I saw, and I tried to do the right thing. They were messing with a murder scene! I saw the other day on *Law & Order—*"

His eyes narrowed at her as he cut her off. "Miss, this is not a game. You've committed a serious crime."

"I didn't make it up!" Clara fought back tears—she was not a crier, but this day kept going from bad to worse.

The detective took a deep breath and let it out slowly. "I think you're a nice girl who watches too much TV. The thing is, dialing 911 and making up a murder is far more serious than just a nuisance call. I've spent hours tracking this down, it took a swarm of officers all afternoon to search the Roman. Not to mention how pissed off your former employer is—a man like Santino Marchetti does not take lightly his guests being inconvenienced."

"Santino? Mr. Marchetti's first name is Santino?"

"Odd, huh? Damn Italians. Listen, Miss Denton, I have to take you into custody and book you. Between us, it's probably just going to be a misdemeanor. You'll post bail and most likely be back home by bedtime."

Clara sniffed hard, fighting the tears, pushing down the panic. "I-I don't have a dime right now. My credit cards are maxed, my bank account is overdrawn, I just lost my job."

The door to the tiny apartment opened and her roommate walked in, his eyes wide at the sight of police. "What's going on?"

She shrugged. "I don't even know anymore."

"Well this guy is right behind me looking for you."

Behind Landon, in the doorway, he stood. Clara's eyes met his; the spark from his ethereal blue eyes caused a stir deep within her. *He was the owner of the Roman? Her boss?*

"Gentlemen, I appreciate your hard work today. It seems this is all just an unfortunate misunderstanding." Clara couldn't focus on Santino's words—the sight of him, standing in her crappy apartment in his fancy suit, the five-o-clock shadow across his chin and cheeks, the way his black hair had that one errant piece that dipped over his right eye—it was more than she could process. *Why did he have to be so beautiful?*

"Misunderstanding?" she asked in unison with the police officers.

"It seems some members of my security detail were playing a prank on a new hire. A silicone body from our Cirque show was placed in one of the rooms, they meant for the new guy to find it, but someone forgot to put out the Do Not Disturb sign. Poor Clara here, I'm afraid, found it first." Santino said the words as if they were final; he was the kind of man that no one questioned.

The detective stood up, confused. "Why the hell didn't anyone bother to tell us this while we were searching your hotel?"

Santino pursed his lips. Clara somehow knew he was thinking up a lie. "My gentlemen were worried they would be reprimanded by me—and they have been. Firing this fine employee was a further effort to cover their wrong-doing."

Able to breathe again, to think again, she leaned back into the chair. *A prank? The body wasn't real?*

Santino moved closer, squatting in front of her on the floor. He was so near that she could smell his cologne as he said, "I am sorry, Clara, for everything."

She struggled to speak, but all that came out was a nod. The room was silent, the strange energy between them electric.

"This whole thing cost a lot of time and money," the detective said. "I think it might be best if we go down to the station and discuss this."

Santino's eyes were still on Clara's—he seemed to care little about the trouble they were in.

He showed no change when the detective's phone rang, or when the detective began to stammer into it. "Sir, I-I of course meant no inconvenience to him, it's just this whole thing reeks of..." Santino continued to look into her eyes as the detective spoke again into his phone. "If that's what you'd like us to do, sure."

The detective walked toward the door and signaled to the uniformed officers to follow. "I'll need to write a report, of course, and Miss Denton I'll ask you to stay in town for a few days, but I can see you had no intention of committing a crime. We'll let this go for now. Good day, Mr. Marchetti."

Santino stood and walked toward the door before turning toward Clara again. "Of course, Clara, I'd love for you to come back to work. I brought a small bonus as an apology. Please take all the time off you need to recover from the hassle." From his pocket he pulled out an envelope. Inside, she begged him to come close to her again—when he was near it felt like when she touched the metal part of a shopping cart at Albertsons. There was a shock, a spark, an almost painful jolt of energy she felt from this man. Instead, he placed the envelope on her battered dining table and left.

Clara didn't move. Not even when Landon placed his hand on her shoulder and asked, "Are you alright, kid?" She simply nodded. Landon always called her "kid" despite the fact that she was six months older.

She didn't move when Landon picked the envelope up from the table and turned it over in his hands. "Classy paper—thick, beefy like that Santiago's cock must be," he teased with a raunchy gesture.

"Santino," she said. "His name is Santino. Earlier I ran out of gas, he helped me. I had no idea who he was."

"Well, that sizzling hunk of a man could not keep his eyes off my little ol' Clara."

"What? No, he—"

"I saw what I saw, baby girl. Maybe he does threesomes."

"Stop it, don't say that." Clara surprised herself, she was jealous of a man she'd only just met, a man whom she would probably never see again; a man who would never look twice at a poor stringy haired college student like herself. "I'm sure he dates models," she said, the thought making her feel nauseous.

Landon ripped open the envelope, which didn't surprise her. He was like that—the kind of guy who got away with anything from their small circle of friends. "Your day is about to get a lot less shitty," he said with an ear-to-ear smile, the kind that made the dimples emerge on his flawless cheeks.

"Did he write me a note?" Her heart skipped a beat as she reached for the envelope. *Did he like her? Did he feel it too?*

"No, but your middle-school crush on the unattainable billionaire boyfriend is cute. It's a check— and we're about to go *out*."

"Severance pay?"

"No," he said, handing her the check.

"Ho-ly crap!" Clara jumped to her feet. "This is, this is, this is..."

"*That* is five thousand dollars. Get dressed, Clara Belle, we're eating well tonight."

Two

---※---

That evening, he sat on his balcony, his mind restless. On his way to the maid's apartment, a cordial call to the chief of police, whom he often quietly let use the hotel's best suite to meet with his mistress, a madam from one of the prominent Pahrump brothels, was enough to get the police to back off.

But what truly troubled him was that he couldn't stop thinking about Clara Denton. Her pale lips when they turned up at the edges into a smile, her slender frame, the sparkle in her brown eyes. What started as damage control had turned into a true attraction, which surprised, and worried, him.

"I'll leave her alone," he said aloud, trying to convince himself. "Nicco will have to do it."

Within twenty minutes, he'd pulled out his MacBook and Googled her. Nothing he saw surprised him—she was raised lower middle-class in North Las Vegas, did well in school, didn't seem to play any sports or engage in group activities. Her stepfather, now unemployed, had been a Blackjack dealer and her mother, now in rehab, was a cocktail waitress. Her biological father died when she was a child, and her mother remarried when Clara was twelve. She was an only child. There were a few pictures on her Facebook profile, none recent, but he printed them off anyway. He'd gained little more information that he had when he'd looked at her employee file earlier that day.

"Why do you have this pull on me?" he said to the image of her on his screen. To Santino, humans were fine to fuck, but nothing more. In the hundreds of years after he'd been made eternal, he'd rarely engaged with any human on an emotional level. But this girl—he couldn't get her out of his head.

He closed the laptop and scanned the airwaves, letting his mind wander as he focused on Clara's image. Unable to read her thoughts, he received one piece of information about her—she was downstairs, at that moment. He inhaled deeply, desperate to smell her, but could not.

Santino stood at the side of the busy downstairs restaurant. Prime & Thyme was located on the ground level, next to the designer shops. For the upscale Roman, it was the more affordable dinner option and had a pub-like atmosphere compared to the five-star Gordon's where he usually dined.

He sat down at the corner of the bar and ordered a drink. The bartender slid him a Scotch, unaware that he was serving the owner of the hotel. As Santino sipped the amber liquid he scanned the seating area.

It took only seconds for him to see her. His pulse, or what functioned as a pulse of sorts, quickened when he saw her. Clara was laughing—he smiled to see her happy. The young human wasn't his type—humans in general didn't interest him beyond the shallow pleasure of vulgar sex that he was able to engage in. The Code that he lived by, along with the other members of his coven, or family as he preferred to call it, had little tolerance for his kind mixing with humans more than casually.

Even for a quick romp, she wasn't his type. If they'd passed each other in the hallway, he wouldn't have taken a second look. But from their first contact when she'd run out of gas, before he knew who she was, he felt something. There was no denying that he was drawn to this human.

Clara felt off that evening, despite being out with her friends at the nicest restaurant she'd been to in ages. Being in the Roman out of uniform felt decadent, but despite Landon convincing her to cash Santino's check and take them both out to dinner, she couldn't bring herself to pass up the employee discount. Besides, she smelled Prime & Thyme every day as she walked behind it to work—and it always smelled heavenly. Halfway through dinner, however, she felt a strange presence—almost like the pressure change before a storm.

Clara's back was to him so she didn't see the suited presence watching them from the corner of the bar, but Landon did. When Santino walked out, Landon said, "I need to use the little boy's room, Clara Bell."

He followed Santino out the front entrance of the casino, as Santino expected him to. Landon's thoughts were easy for even Santino to read. The roommate had been waiting for an hour for Santino to use the restroom—but Santino never really *needed* to use the restroom. Instead, he decided to let the annoying boy confront him outside.

"You didn't need to buy her off, buddy. Clara believed you."

As he lit his Marlboro, Santino turned to see Landon standing next to him, as he expected.

"It was simply an apology, nothing more. The incident was handled poorly."

"Can I bum a smoke?" Landon asked.

Santino held the pack out and lit the cigarette when it was dangling from Landon's lower lip.

"You are her boyfriend?" Santino searched the mind of the young man as he inhaled the cigarette.

"No, I'm available," Landon said as he exhaled. Leaning into Santino, he whispered, "and you're exactly my type."

"You couldn't handle me, boy," Santino said, his lips inches from Landon's. With a grin, he thought, *You have no idea what my cock would do to you.*

"Your eyes seem to be all over my girl," Landon said with a nod toward Clara.

Santino looked deeply into Landon's eyes—his thoughts were transparent, even for a horrible mind reader like himself. Landon Miller and Clara Denton were friends, nothing more.

When Landon turned to ask Santino to join them, he was gone like a puff of their cigarette smoke.

He decided not to tell Clara—he didn't want her chasing some guy she'd never get anywhere with. Even hours later, when the waitress said the bill had been paid by some "guy in a suit," Landon simply shrugged.

* * * * *

The next day at work, she felt him before she saw him. When Santino Marchetti was near, it was as if the ions around her became supercharged—her palms went sweaty, her stomach tied itself into a bow, and her heart raced. The sound of his voice caused her to jolt and drop her cleaning basket on the plush carpet.

"I didn't mean to alarm you, Clara." He walked over toward her and knelt down to clean up the sprawled contents of the basket.

"Mr. Marchetti," was all she could manage to squeak out. He stood and set the basket on the desk.

"Call me Santino, please. We're friends now, are we not?"

She nodded, confused and more than a little nervous. The suited presence of Santino, while she stood there cleaning a dirty hotel room in her uniform, made her feel fidgety, afraid.

"I didn't expect you back to work so soon."

Unable to form words, she awkwardly stared at him until he spoke again, the deep lull of his voice calming her a little. "Have you had lunch?"

"Um, no, I mean—I work today from ten to three."

He reached out a hand to her. "Do allow me the pleasure of your company, Clara. I was just headed up to Gordon's to dine."

She blinked fast. *Was this really happening?*

"I'm part time, I don't get a lunch break." He glanced around the room, his hand still stretched in her direction.

"Fortunately," he said with a grin, "I know your boss, and he thinks it will be fine. You are hungry, Clara, I've heard your stomach growl twice. Come now."

She took his hand; a jolt of electricity arched through her at his touch.

"Uh, okay, but, um Gordon's is closed for lunch I think." He walked her out of the half-cleaned room and down the long hallway, her hand in his.

"They open exclusively for me, Miss Denton. You are full of excuses this afternoon."

"Well, it's just, I should tell my shift supervisor that—"

"Indeed. I value your work ethic—I shall have my assistant notify the appropriate staff that you are taking the rest of your shift off with full pay."

Santino's private table at the elegant five-star restaurant, Gordon's Steakhouse, overlooked the Strip. He loved the hustle and bustle of daily life here in this strange city that he had made his home, for now, until he'd be forced to move on. The family was *always* forced to move on, eventually.

When the waiter appeared with water, Santino waved his hand at the table and said, "Bring us a bit of whatever is ready."

The waiter turned to leave, and Santino added, "Oh, and Reginald, bring me a bottle of that Bryant Cabernet that just came in."

"Yes, sir," Reginald answered as he headed toward the back of the elegant restaurant.

"I-I can't really drink. I mean, I'm still working and I have to drive home and all."

He didn't answer.

They sat in silence until Reginald returned with the wine, pouring a small sample into Santino's glass for approval. With a nod, the waiter filled both their glasses and left the bottle on the white-linen clad table.

Clara nervously broke the silence. "Listen, Mr. Marchetti—"

"Santino."

"Uh, yeah, listen Santino—if this is about what happened yesterday, there's no need. I really appreciate you letting me keep my job, because I really need this job, but you don't have to buy me lunch. It was a misunderstanding, I get that now."

"This," he said with the wave of his hand across the table, "is about the fact that it is my mid-day meal time, the same as every day. You are my guest merely because you are hungry." With a slow sip of his wine, he signaled to Reginald that he was ready for bread.

"Well," Clara stammered, reaching for the heavy crystal glass. "I mean, then, why were you in the room I was cleaning in the first place?" She took a tentative sip of the dense red wine. The soothing warmth from it flowed down her throat.

"Miss Denton, I don't understand why you are surprised at my presence at your workplace. I'm not sure if you are aware, but I own this hotel." He smiled at her, something so rare for him that he was immediately self-conscious of it and forced his lips to return to a straight line.

Santino's eyes found hers. This girl intrigued him. Clara Denton seemed to most onlookers like a shrinking violet, timid even. But he saw more—under the lack of confidence she was strong and driven. He sensed it, and rarely was Santino in tune with humans. His best friend, Nicco, understood them, but Santino did not.

"Point taken," she chuckled, taking another hearty sip of the wine. "Of course I've worked here for nearly a year and have never seen you before, certainly not walking down the hall of the least expensive block of rooms."

The wine was making her bold, but her hand shook as she realized she was engaging in flirty banter with *the* Santino Marchetti.

"A fair point. I will confess that I wanted to ensure that you were not disturbed any further by yesterday's events."

She began to answer, but stopped as the waiter placed a basket of bread on the table. Clara's stomach howled as she smelled the heavenly odor of freshly baked bread.

Santino's pale eyes studied her once again. He reached for the breadbasket and held it in front of Clara. "Thank you," she muttered as she grabbed a sourdough roll.

"Clara, do you feel okay," she heard him say, but everything was hazy.

"Oh, um, I'm sorry Mr. M- um, Mr. Mar- Oh God I feel dizzy." She tried to stand from the chair but fell back down. The restaurant was spinning.

"Do you see why you shouldn't skip meals?" His voice was at her ear, but oddly muffled.

"I-I guess so," was all she could manage to answer before she slid from the chair.

"Reginald, call Vittoria—tell her I'm taking the maid upstairs. Have her send for Dr. Arnaud immediately."

Clara could hear him, but was unable to make sense of much. Her entire focus was on staying conscious, but within minutes she was in a deep sleep.

He scooped her up and carried her in his arms to the private elevator at the rear of the hallway and up to his penthouse. Instead of resting her on the sofa, he walked into his own bedroom and sat down on the bed, holding her in his arms. "You'll be fine Clara, the doctor is on his way."

Despite his buzzing phone, he continued to cradle her in his arms. He could hear her normal heartbeat, her breathing, and swore to himself that he would never harm her—that he *didn't* harm her.

"Santino, what the hell?" His assistant, Vittoria Farnese, stood in the doorway of his bedroom minutes later. He gently placed Clara's weak head on his pillow and slid out from under her. "A reaction to...to lunch," he said with a nod toward the door.

"Dr. Arnaud is in the living room, he's not comfortable coming into your bed chamber."

Santino exhaled hard. "That damn superstitious warlock! Stay with her, I need to talk to him before he examines her."

Vittoria looked at Clara on the bed. In *his* bed. *How dare he bring her here, sick or not—he was breaking all the rules—his rules.* Clara moaned, and Vittoria leaned in, unsure of what to do. She reached down and pulled the maid's shoes off and covered her with a cashmere throw blanket from the end of the bed. She could hear Santino beyond the door arguing with the doctor.

"I need to know what you gave to her. She could have an allergy or reaction, something like that. It might be best to just drop her at a public emergency room."

"No, Pierre," Santino said through gritted teeth, "that cannot happen."

"So this is it, Scopolamine?"

"Yes, doctor. I've used it before on the opaque mind, but never with this reaction."

"Okay, I'll treat her, but out here."

"I should break your Creole neck, Pierre—what do you think is in there? A fucking coffin?" Dr. Pierre Arnaud feared Santino—he feared all the blood drinkers—but they were all he had after being condemned to die by his own kind. Still, he refused to damn his own soul to hell by entering Santino's bedroom.

"Fine," Santino snapped. "Vittoria," he yelled, "bring her out here."

Vittoria lifted the maid, still wrapped in the cashmere throw, from the bed and effortlessly carried her to the living room. "Gently," Santino scolded as he moved to assist her in lying Clara on the sofa.

As the doctor lowered his stethoscope to Clara's chest, Santino looked to Vittoria. "This is none of your business."

"Clearly," she snapped. "I'll get the driver to have the car ready to take her home."

"No, I'll do it. I have a conference call in twenty minutes with Rome. Retrieve the notes from my desk and handle it." Santino's eyes drifted nervously back to Clara—the doctor was taking her pulse.

"Me? Deal with *them*? While you do what, sir, babysit *her*?"

"Vittoria, obey me, now."

She stormed from his penthouse, slamming the door behind her.

"Firecracker," the doctor said with a whistle.

27

"Indeed," Santino said as he collapsed into the chair opposite them.

"Well, listen boss—I think the maid is fine. She's thin, probably had an empty stomach, not much of a drinker most likely—I think it just hit her a little harder than you're used to."

"You're sure?" Santino was relieved.

"If she's not back to normal in an hour, call me." The doctor looked anxiously around the penthouse—he'd never been inside Santino's private residence before and it made him nervous to be there. "May I go?"

"Yes, Pierre. And thank you for your assistance this afternoon."

Santino sat in the chair watching her sleep. When she rolled over and pulled the blanket around her, she reminded him of an angel—the sweet kind, not the dark kind that roamed the rural areas looking for evil.

"This is soft, I love this blanket," she said. Her eyes were still closed, but her hand was stroking the cashmere.

"Clara, are you awake?"

"A little, I think."

"Is everything okay?"

"I think so, yeah."

"How do you feel about me?"

"Um," she said sleepily, "I like you a lot."

"Good. We are friends then? You and I?"

"Yes," she said, rolling over.

"The other day, when you found the—"

Something changed in that instant—Clara suddenly felt awake.

"Where am I?" She sat up, her eyelids straining to open.

"You are in my home, Clara. You became ill during our lunch. Do you remember?"

"I remember eating bread, and then...did I drink too much wine? I'm so sorry if I did, I don't normally do that. Maybe my body isn't used to the good stuff."

He smiled at her. "Maybe. Let me get you some water."

* * * * *

"Rome is full of vipers," Vittoria huffed from behind his desk as he walked in.

"I know, I'm sorry about that. I had to tend to the girl." Santino reached for the notes from her phone meeting and glanced at them. "You seemed to handle them quite capably," he admitted, flipping to the second page. "Better than I would have done."

"The she-devil scares me—but I tried to stand our ground."

"Octavia can try even the most patient souls."

Vittoria glanced at her watch. "Did you drive the maid home already? You must not have gotten very far with her."

"No, she refused. She's finishing her shift at the moment." Santino felt a sense of loss that he didn't get to spend more time with Clara that afternoon.

"I'll talk to Nicco again—maybe he can get somewhere with her."

"No," Santino snapped.

Vittoria stared at him.

"I'm sorry, I'm edgy today. This whole thing has me rattled, but I alone will deal with Clara Denton."

Three

He was known as the Hunter. Matthew sped down the desolate, dry pavement of I-15 toward Las Vegas. Just before the famous traffic-clogged travel artery known locally as the Spaghetti Bowl, Matthew's 1989 Ford F-150 began to sputter like a lifetime smoker after a mile-long walk around Walmart.

Matthew stepped on the gas and shifted, struggling to keep the truck alive until he could get to his aunt's house in the posh Las Vegas suburbs. The truck sputtered, but kept going—past the Strip it staggered, down Interstate 15, known locally as "the fifteen," toward the southern branch of Henderson.

When he arrived, she tried to feed him as aunts always do. Despite his half-hearted resistance, it was flank steak after all, he sat down at her oak dining room table to a meal. Matthew glanced at his phone as his Aunt Janet prattled on about Henderson, road construction around the Metro area, and his mother, her sister, Dawn.

"Yes, Aunt Jan, she's doing better on the blood thinners."

"And your father? He always was an odd duck. Gordon Vance Hunter, conspiracy theorist, we used to call him in high school." His aunt shoveled lumpy mashed potatoes onto his plate as he tried to defend his father.

"Dad, he's good, slowing down for sure. But, Aunt Jan, he's not insane. You would be shocked at what walks among us, disguised as human, even here in Las Vegas."

Aunt Jan leveled her eyes at her nephew. She loved her sister's son, but she feared his father's madness had tainted him. "Lots of wild things here in Vegas," she said with a wink, "just head down to Fremont Street after dark."

Matthew smiled. "Good point. Thank you again for letting me stay. I hope I'm not an imposition."

"Never," she said, plopping another scoop of starchy potatoes on his plate.

Later that night, in the privacy of the guest room of his aunt's upscale Henderson home, Matthew Hunter pulled out his laptop and tapped in the Wi-Fi code she'd given him. With a few strokes, he was logged into his blog. *The Hunter* had 500,000 followers—followers who believed in him. Followers who bought the books he put out in the indie paranormal world, books many critics discounted as "trash." His monthly publications didn't make much money, despite the volume he sold, due to their 99-cent price tag, but the social media following gave him a rush like nothing he'd ever felt before.

I am on the trail, my fellow seekers, he typed into the auto-posting app he used to keep his myriad of fans updated on his quest. Within seconds, the post to his Facebook profile had a hundred likes and half as many comments. The attention filled him, almost made him forget the nerdy, bullied boy he'd been in high school.

He looked again at his tattered leather-bound notebook. *Clara Denton*, his handwritten notes read. *UNLV student, reported a body at the Roman,* he read back to himself. "Tomorrow, Clara, we'll meet," he said aloud in the modest guest room.

* * * * *

Clara was late: late and rattled. The whole situation at the Roman, with Santino, was so odd, and so *exciting*, that she couldn't focus. As she rushed toward her car, she froze when she saw him standing there. He was her type; there was no doubt. Floppy blond hair cascaded over his forehead as he swiped at his phone. When his eyes met hers, she melted a little; blue eyes so deep that she was entranced for several long moments. He was leaning on her car; this cute guy in a polo shirt, khakis, Docksider shoes and all. He even carried a battered leather messenger bag across his chest.

"Can I help you?" she asked casually.

"Clara Denton?"

"That's me."

"I'm Matthew Hunter. I was hoping for a word?"

"Oh, I'm late for work. I made the car payment yesterday if that's what this is about—I have a receipt on my phone. Let me find..."

"Clara, I'm here about the body you found at the Roman the other day. I'm sure you've heard of my blog—*The Hunter*?"

"Uh, no, but that was all a misunderstanding the other day. I guess I got a little too caught up in the Blood Lust Killings."

He nodded and leaned toward her, confident that he'd found his way in. "I'm investigating the serial killer, don't tell anyone," he whispered.

And he was right—she was interested. "It's all over the news," she said in excitement.

"Well, I sort of am the news. I'd love to interview you—maybe over dinner tonight?"

She thought of Santino and how hard he was trying to keep her quiet. She glanced at her watch. "I really am late. It was nice meeting you, Matthew."

"Maybe later then, it really is important. Here's my card." He handed her a business card that she shoved in her pocket.

"I didn't know people still did cards," she said as she opened her car door.

"Please, Clara, give me a call. Your safety depends on it."

"Sure," she said, having no intention of contacting the strange but cute blond.

But, after work that day, her curiosity got the better of her. She searched Matthew Hunter and found his blog—despite his oddness, he seemed legit and had a fairly large following. At around six, gazing at the empty fridge in her apartment, she decided to see what he had to say. She texted him to meet her at Joey's Pizzeria at seven and hoped he'd buy.

When she arrived, he was nervously swiping at his phone. Only a glass of water sat in front of him. "Hi Matthew," she said, sliding into the red vinyl booth across from him. "You came," he said, as surprised as she was at her presence.

"I said I would. Thanks for dinner." The awkwardness of two socially inept people having dinner hung in the dry Las Vegas air. He nodded, glancing at the menu and doing the math as to what this dinner would cost him.

"Can we cut to the chase? What do you want from me?"

His eyes shot to hers. His heart pounded for a second before he willed it to behave—she was pretty. Not beautiful, not attention getting, but just quietly pretty. "Okay, can we talk about the dead body you reported at the Roman?"

"Oh, that," she said with the wave of her hand. "A big misunderstanding."

"Misunderstanding, right." His eyes went back to his menu. Matthew had a hundred dollars credit left on his Visa. He hoped that evening wouldn't max out his card.

"How did you know? They dropped the charges against me."

"I have a vast network of contacts," he said with a proud smirk.

"I'm excited that you're interested in the Blood Lust Killer, that's why I came, to be honest. I love True Crime novels."

"I'm on his trail," he said, the edges of his lips curving upward into a grin.

"I can't stop following it!"

"Well, Clara, it seems you are now right in the middle of it."

"Can I take your order?"

Matthew and Clara looked up at the aproned figure of Landon standing at the edge of their table. She smiled at her roommate. "I think we'll share the pepperoni extreme," she said, glancing to Matthew for approval. He nodded as she continued, "A pitcher of Sangria, and the gooey parm bread."

Landon wrote in his notebook and smiled at Clara. "On the way."

"That waiter was flirting with you," Matthew said with a quick glance to his phone. His Instagram was blowing up at the suggestion that he was dining with a witness to a Blood Lust murder.

"He wasn't," she confessed. "He's my roommate. More likely he was flirting with you."

"I don't understand."

"Never mind. Listen, Matthew, I appreciate dinner, but I don't really have any information about the serial killings at all."

"The body you found at the Roman—it was real; real *and* covered up. Tell me what you saw."

"Oh, no, that...my boss, Santino, said that it was a prank from the crew at the—"

"The body was real, Clara. Your boss lied about it. Covered it up to protect the murderer."

"Why would he do that?"

"Because," Matthew said with a sip of the sweet Sangria Landon had set down seconds prior, "the murderer is either Mr. Marchetti, or one of his kind."

"His *kind?*"

* * * * *

She couldn't stop thinking about her conversation with Matthew Hunter. Clara had left abruptly the night before, as soon as he'd paid for their dinner. At first she was entertained by his knowledge of the killings, but when he took it a step further, she became concerned. *He's crazy,* she'd realized as they polished off the pitcher of Sangria. *Cute, but utterly insane. A grown man who still believed in vampires?*

At around ten, Landon came home and riffled through the cabinets. "There's nothing to drink," he moaned.

"Oh, I bought milk earlier, help yourself."

"I mean to drink. Today was hell at work—an entire baseball league came in. Middle-schoolers, they were even throwing meatballs at each other. I need to drink it away and then dance. What do ya say, Clara Bell? Take me out?"

She closed her Word document—there were three days before her paper was due. Clara wasn't much of a dancer, but she welcomed the distraction that night. Thoughts of bodies, killings, vampires, and lunatic bloggers were making her head hurt.

"Sure, but let's stay far from the Roman," she insisted.

"Whatever you say, baby girl."

But, within an hour, they sat at the lively Pulse Lounge just off the gaming tables at her place of employment. "Usually you want to use the discount," Landon argued when she protested.

"Tonight I didn't," she said with an eye roll.

"C'mon, girl, the bartender here wants in my pants—I need to see and be seen."

Santino couldn't stay away from this mortal female. From the corner of the crowded dance club, he sat watching her. She was happy, smiling. Clara sat at tiny table with her roommate, Landon Miller. She was dressed simply—jeans, leather ballet flats, and a black t-shirt, but he sensed this was the best she had for a night out. Clara's lips were coated with lipgloss and they glistened as she laughed.

Santino had been watching her for over two hours, ever since his head of security notified him that the target was once again on the property. He watched as her roommate left with one of his more popular bartenders, not bothering to tell Clara that he was leaving. Santino could tell she was sitting there waiting for his return, nursing a bottle of cheap beer.

When she looked at her phone and signaled to the waitress that she was ready to settle their tab, Santino made his move. Despite his careful calculation of Clara's alcohol intake, he convinced himself that she shouldn't drive herself home. He texted his assistant Vittoria to meet him at Clara's car in the employee parking garage.

"Common courtesy, caring for our staff," he said as Vittoria arrived at the car. She shook her head in disbelief as he ran his hand over the hood of Clara's car—with a sudden surge, an electrical charge from his brain through his fingers to the battery—he rendered it useless.

"Clear her bar tab and tell me when she walks down," he said, pulling his own keys from his suit pocket.

Clara cringed when the waitress brought the bill. It was fun to have a night out, despite Landon ditching her for the cute bartender guy, but two hundred dollars seemed excessive. She had the money from Santino's check, but she intended to use that to pay down bills, not to live it up. Landon never understood—he grew up with money, and even now that his family had disowned him, he still lived like lack of funds was a temporary setback.

"Oh, is my employee discount on here? It's twenty percent, right?" she asked when the waitress came back.

"Oops, I'll go deduct that," she'd said. But when the waitress came back, she was beaming. "Uh, it's been paid—I'm not sure how, but it's showing no balance at all."

Clara stared in disbelief. "I can't leave without paying, I'm sure it's a mistake—do you want my card number just in case?"

The waitress smiled. "No, it looks like the casino comped it; they even left a big tip for me. I'd say it's our lucky day."

But Clara didn't feel lucky when she climbed into her car and turned the key and heard only a metallic click and then nothing. "Not a dead battery, not now," she begged, as if the car could respond. Tired and hungry, she opened the driver's door and peered around the parking garage. It was late, but she hoped there was still an attendant somewhere who could help her with a jump—for free, she prayed.

As she rounded the corner of the row of cars, she heard his tires screech. Once again, the black Maserati came dangerously close to her. This time, however, as she looked up at the tinted windshield, she knew who she would see.

Santino shifted the car into park and stepped out. "Well, if it isn't my friend Clara Denton," he said.

She looked around the garage—they were alone. "Uh, yeah, I know I'm not supposed to park in this lot when I'm not working—it's just that big show is going on and the self-park was full, so I—"

"Clara I assure you it's fine. Is there a problem with your vehicle? Out of gas again, perhaps?"

She felt her skin burn—she wasn't sure if he was angry or simply teasing her.

"It's my battery, it seems to be dead."

"Dead?"

"Uh, it won't start. Can you maybe give me a jump?" she asked with a cringe.

"I'd love to jump you Clara, but unfortunately lack the proper equipment to do such a thing." He walked around the car and opened the passenger door. "Please, get in. I will take you home while the maintenance staff tends to your vehicle."

He was sexy in his suit, standing next to his sports car, but she couldn't help but think of what Matthew Hunter said—it was crazy, yes, but there was something about this guy that was different, otherworldly almost. Getting in a car with him seemed foolhardy, and yet, when he gestured once again for her to get inside, she did.

"Oh they'll need my car key," she said when he joined her in the car.

"They will figure it out." He shifted out of park and stepped on the gas, barreling through the garage until they were flying down the exit ramp.

She nervously sent Landon a text—she wanted someone to know that she was alone in the car with the mysterious Santino Marchetti.

"How are you feeling? I've been concerned since you became ill at lunch," he asked, glancing in the rearview mirror as he cut through three lanes to turn onto Las Vegas Boulevard.

"Oh, yeah, that, I'm fine. I think it was just the wine on an empty stomach. I'm sorry I ruined your meal."

"Your company was refreshing, Clara, for the short time that it lasted. Perhaps tonight we shall make it to a second course." Santino looked over his shoulder and cut through the line of taxis into an underground ramp.

"Uh, tonight, what? Mr. Marchetti, where are we going?"

"Santino."

"Uh, yeah, Santino—where are we going? My friend is waiting for me." A moment of terror struck her—she'd gotten into a car at two in the morning with a man she barely knew as a serial killer preyed on the women of Las Vegas. And now, to make it even worse, they'd pulled into some private underground structure.

"Your roommate is quite preoccupied with my bartender and will be for some time. You're hungry, so I thought we might make a quick stop at the Supper Club."

"Supper Club? I've never heard of that."

"For members only, but the cuisine is quite authentic," he explained as they pulled up to a steel door. The door opened, and she was relieved when a uniformed valet emerged and guided them from the car into the restaurant.

"They serve food this late?" she whispered to Santino as a hostess in a long black taffeta dress escorted them to a private booth in the rear of the dark dining room.

"Time is relative," he answered, signaling to the waitress.

Clara looked around—there were a few other diners, all dressed formally.

"I'm underdressed as usual," she said as the waitress approached.

"Nonsense."

"Well that guy in the corner is staring at me like I'm a freak."

"In the corner? You see something?"

"Yeah, that bearded guy in the old-timey suit is glaring at me."

"You see him, interesting," Santino said with a glance to the corner where Clara had gestured—he saw nothing.

When the waitress arrived he spoke to her in another language. There were no menus, and no one asked what she wanted.

As the waitress left to bring wine, he glanced at the incredulous Clara. "I apologize for my rudeness—they only speak my language, and serve whatever the matron of the family feels like preparing."

"Oh," Clara said as he filled her wineglass from the carafe.

"I don't know much about wine," she confessed. "But this is really good."

"Good wine is a good familiar creature," Santino said absently, draining his glass.

"If it be well used," she answered quickly, completing the quote from *Othello*.

He leveled his eyes at her—she was intelligent, and nothing intrigued him more than intelligent humans. They were becoming more and more scarce as the years wore on.

"You are quite unique," he said, signaling to the waitress to bring the food.

As she finished her pasta, he hoped the second carafe of wine would loosen her tongue. "So, has anyone been bothering you about...anything?"

"Oh, you mean the thing the other day? No."

"No one at all?" He knew she was lying to him.

"Well some nutso blog guy tried to ask me questions. The Hunter or something—have you ever heard of him?"

"No," he lied. "But I'd stay very far away from types like that. If he tries to contact you again, let me know. I'll take care of him."

After dessert, Santino glanced at his watch. "It's nearly three-thirty my lovely Clara. I'd best get you home."

"Uh, should you drive after all that wine?"

"Wine has no effect on me whatsoever. Come now," he said, sliding from the booth and reaching out a hand for her. They left, and to her surprise, there was no bill, although when the valet delivered his car, Santino did tip him.

As they pulled into her apartment complex, it began to sprinkle. "It's raining," Clara squealed.

"So it is." Santino turned on his windshield wipers and looked out the window as the sprinkle turned into a shower. "You do know what this means, right?"

She shook her head and answered, "Well, it's monsoon season of course."

"Miss Denton, there is no other option but for us to dance in the rain."

She looked over at him with a wide grin—his face glowed from the dashboard lights. "How very old-fashioned," she said with a nod.

"I'm an old-fashioned guy. One dance, and I shall walk you to your door like a perfect gentleman."

"Deal," she answered as he started the music. "Not too modern now," she teased as Frank Sinatra crooned through the speakers.

He climbed out of the driver's seat, leaving his door open as he walked around the car and opened her door, holding out his right hand for her.

"Santino, seriously though, you'll ruin that expensive suit," she argued as he walked her to the front of the car.

He looked at her in the flood of the headlights. "A suit can easily be replaced, Clara, but this evening will never come again. May I have this dance?"

She took his hand, and in the parking lot of her cheap apartment complex, she drew close to him as they swayed to *Strangers In The Night*. "I bet that guy would have been so cool to hang out with," she said as he pulled her closer.

"Frank? He was," Santino said with a sigh.

"What?" she asked, drawing closer to him as the warm rain soaked them both.

"Nothing." He leaned into her, resisting the urge to push too far. "You are so beautiful tonight, Clara. So alive—I love seeing you like this."

45

The song ended, and yet they clung to each other for several long moments until another car pulled into the parking lot. His eyes met hers. "Allow me to turn off the car and I'll walk you to your door."

"Okay," she said, feeling drunk, but not from her earlier imbibing. She was drunk on Santino Marchetti.

When they stood at her door, she didn't want the night to end. "Uh," she hesitated, pushing the metal door open with her key, "do you want to come in?"

His index finger brushed across her cheek. "I had best not. Goodnight, Clara."

*****

"Well did he kiss you?" Landon was sitting in front of the TV the following morning, the local weatherperson droning on about wind advisories and turning off your sprinkler system. He shoveled giant spoonfuls of some colorful children's cereal into his mouth as he waited for her answer.

"No, but we danced...in the rain," she said, wrapping her arms around herself, remembering the most romantic dance of her life.

"How very, um, well, stupid," he said, wiping his lips with the back of his hand.

"It was romantic, you butthole."

"Watch your language, baby girl," he teased. "When are you seeing Sexy and Suited again?"

"Oh, I mean, probably never. It wasn't like a date I don't think—it was my boss driving me home when my battery wouldn't start I think. But it was a glorious fantasy for a little while."

"Driving you home, personally, in his Maserati, and then oh, just on a whim, dancing with you in the rain?"

"I-I don't know, really. He even took me to this weird place for dinner, but a guy like that is never going to be with a maid in his hotel." She glanced at her watch. "Crap, I need to get to class—and I have no car—can you give me a ride to campus?"

"No can do, Clara Belle, I have to be at taser training in twenty minutes. It's bus city for you, my love-struck BFF."

As she headed down the stairs, rushing to catch the city bus, she saw her car sitting in her usual parking spot. It had been washed, detailed, and the gas tank was full. She couldn't remember the last time she'd had more than half a tank of gas. When she turned the key and started it up *Strangers In The Night* began to play through her scratchy speakers. She looked down at the archaic sound system and pushed the black button—out popped a cassette tape. Clara was completely baffled as she drove to class. "That's so 80s," she said out loud, "he made me a mix tape."

*****

Early the next morning, her feet barely touched the floor as she glided across the gleaming hardwood floor to slam the china mug down on Santino's desk.

He ignored her.

"You're welcome," she sputtered, falling into the overstuffed leather chair in front of him.

Santino continued to type out his email, reaching over absently to sip the thick, black coffee that she'd brewed to perfection.

After several minutes of her seething, he finally looked over. "Do you have something to say, Vittoria?"

"How could you?" she hissed.

"How could I *what?*" His voice was low, threatening. Santino knew exactly why his assistant was as angry as a disturbed rattlesnake.

She softened, the icy stare wilting her resolve to unleash on him. "How could you fall for a human?"

With a deep breath, he leaned back in his chair. "I haven't fallen," he said, the lie clear to them both.

"You of all people, *mio cuore,*" she said with the shake of her head. Vittoria collected his half empty coffee cup and left the room. His words to her back hung in the dry air: "I'll never be that to you, Vittoria."

Four

Hours later, across town, Clara sat in a stark lobby at the Clark County Detention Center. It was over an hour before she was directed to a booth to speak to him. The person at the desk, after she'd gone through a metal detector and signed in, told her that inmates weren't allowed to have visitors in person, but she could talk to him through a video system.

When she saw his face, she swallowed the tears.

"Hey baby," he said.

"Did they charge you?"

He nodded. "Yeah, third offense too."

"Dad, how could you?"

"I was broke, and tomorrow is her birthday. I saw the pendant at the grocery store while I was buying a pack of Camels—it was a glass butterfly with little colored stones floating inside. You know how Amanda loves butterflies. Included the chain, too."

"You couldn't take the money from the cigarettes and buy it? Did the necklace cost more than a frickin' pack of Camel Crushes?"

Clara shook her head at him. She adored him but he infuriated her—Roy Cooper had loved her like a father since her biological father died, but the decisions both her parents made astounded her.

"It doesn't matter—I was caught and ended up without the necklace or the smokes. Do you think you could get me a pack?"

She leaned back in the plastic chair. "We'll see. Have they said how long they're keeping you?"

"The public defender said it's a minor offense, and they're only being harsh with me because I have prior shoplifting stuff on my record. He thinks this afternoon the judge will set bail at a grand."

She sat silently, debating what to do.

"Clara, baby, I know how strapped you are with school and all, but is there any way you can scrape it up? The bondsman doesn't require that much up front."

She wasn't sure whether to laugh or to cry. "You'll do it again. Why can't you two just get your lives together?"

He sighed and ran his hands through his greased-down hair. "I guess we're not all as smart as you, baby. Your mother's addiction has put us all through hell, but you act like she does it to personally fuck you over. Clara, it doesn't have shit to do with you. Neither did the other thing, but you ball all of it up inside as your doing. She's an addict; she's sick."

"She is an addict and you are a thief."

He nodded. "Yes, I'm a thief. You know what, forget about the bail. This isn't your problem. I'll figure it out. I guess I was desperate to get out of here by tomorrow."

"What's tomorrow?"

He turned red and took a deep breath. He loved her like his own, but Clara could be so focused on making a better life for herself that she often buried everyone who cared for her in the dust. "Your mother's birthday—I just said that a few minutes ago. Did you plan to go see her?"

"No," Clara said flatly. She hadn't seen her mother once during the current ninety-day rehab program she was in.

"Please, Clara, especially if I can't make it out of here in time, go see her on her birthday. Don't hold past sins against her forever—accept her for what she is and love her before it's too late."

Later that afternoon as she got ready for work, she received a text from her stepfather that simply said:

> *Rich bossman posted my bail. This jailbird is free! I'm going out for a drink with the boys— but please come tomorrow. She's still your mom.*

* * * * *

She was on her fourth room when she couldn't take it anymore. Santino Marchetti had gone too far this time. When her supervisor was on a break, she crept down the long hallway and took the service elevator down to the lobby. Against all the employee rules, she walked across the bustling casino floor to the other side of the complex—to the tower where the best suites were. On the floor directly below Santino's penthouse sat his offices. She managed to get as far as the reception area with her ID card.

On the terrazzo tile, she stood in front of the gleaming mahogany reception desk. A perky brunette stared at her, then stared a bit more before Clara began to speak. "I-I know I'm in uniform, but it's just...I really need to speak to Mr. Marchetti."

The brunette laughed—actually laughed at her.

"Um," she said, glancing at the nametag, "Clara, maids aren't really allowed on this floor, you must know that. Now, who is your supervisor?"

"Please, I need to talk to him, just for a second."

"Right," the receptionist chirped, "security it is then." Clara looked around the expansive lobby as the bitchy receptionist phoned security to have her removed.

They both froze when he walked out, the click of his heels on the gleaming tile the only sound in the room. "Jenna, that will not be necessary. Please inform Miss Denton's supervisor that I've called her away from her duties this afternoon to assist me with a project."

The receptionist, Jenna he called her, hung up the phone and stared at the waif-like maid in front of her. The boss rarely spoke to her, and had never walked across the lobby to meet a visitor, *any* visitor.

"Jenna, are we clear?"

"Oh, um, yes, yes sir, I mean, yes Mr. Marchetti."

She stood in front of him as he leaned on his desk, puzzled but delighted that she was there. "To what do I owe this wonderful surprise?"

"I don't need you to rescue me."

"Rescue you? Why ever would you need that?"

"I know I'm messed up, I know sometimes I can't afford to buy bread, and I know that my car is falling apart, and I know that to you I'm the epitome of North Las Vegas white trash, but I am *not* a damsel in distress, Mr. Marchetti."

"So we're back to Mr. Marchetti, are we? No, Miss Denton, you are not in need of rescue. You, Clara, are a smart, resourceful, strong, and very beautiful woman. And furthermore, I am in no condition to rescue anyone—I'm as broken as they come. So what is this about?"

"You paid the bail money, right? At the jail today?" *He said I'm beautiful,* she thought.

"You were in jail? I talked to the chief, that false police report has all been settled."

"No, not me. My father."

"Sit, please." He gestured to the leather sofa at the side of the office.

"You gave me that huge check, and then the other night, with my dead battery, and now *this.*"

"Ah," he said, sitting next to her. "So my heinous crimes are feeling remorse that you were so terribly inconvenienced while under my employ that I wanted to make it right, and then I was monstrous enough to drive you home when your car was in need of maintenance. And now, you believe I've bailed your father out of jail?"

"He's my stepfather. And well, I mean, I can see that you were trying to help but he keeps doing this and someone always bails him out then they give him a slap on the wrist."

"Clara," he said, reaching for her hand, "this is a misunderstanding. I had no knowledge of your family member's brush with the law."

"Oh," she said, looking down at his hand on hers. The second his skin had touched hers, the spark went off again. "I'm sorry, I-I feel like an idiot."

"You are not an idiot, but you are hungry. Have you had dinner?"

"Um, no, but it's fine, you don't need to—"

"As we agreed a few minutes ago, I don't need to. But I'd love to have dinner with you."

"Oh," she said again, "Um, I'm not really dressed for dinner here at the Roman."

"I own the Roman, and my guests dress however they choose."

"I wouldn't say this is anything I would choose," she joked.

He smiled at her—the sound of her laugh, the shine of her smile, the feel of her skin—there was something magical about this young woman. "If you're uncomfortable, we'll order in. We can dine on my terrace if you'd like?"

"Oh."

"Oh," he teased. "I can have a chaperone watch us dine if it would set you at ease?"

"No, uh, yeah, thank you. Dinner would be cool."

* * * * *

Santino clicked a button on his desk and said into the intercom system, "Vittoria can you come in here please."

Clara pointed toward the door and mouthed "bathroom."

"Use mine if you'd like," he said, gesturing toward a door at the side of the office.

His masculine bathroom was as elegant as the rest of the office. There was even a shower and a walk-in closet. As she washed her hands, she could hear them arguing.

"You want me to *what?* In your *penthouse?* Santino please, give this some thought."

"I have. Arrange dinner on the terrace and make it stellar. That will be all—first course exactly at seven."

"Let me arrange one of the suites where you can..."

"No! Not with her. Get it done, and fast. Make sure we're alone after dessert is served."

When she heard Vittoria's heels click out of the office and the door slam, Clara emerged from the bathroom.

"It doesn't sound like your assistant is happy about our dinner."

"It doesn't matter," he answered, reaching a hand to Clara. "I am happy about it, but could you indulge me for about half an hour? I have a short meeting before I can call it a day. The receptionist will give you a player's card—would that keep you occupied?"

She stared at him and nodded as she left his office.

She passed his assistant, Vittoria, who glared at her through her opened office door. She was on the phone—arranging dinner.

The receptionist called after her as she passed the desk, reminding her that Mr. Marchetti wanted her to take a loaded player's card. "Play all you want with this, it's like an unlimited credit card—just swipe it in the machines," she'd explained. "You won't cash out, it's just for fun."

Clara was overwhelmed by it all, and for a split second thought about leaving, but she couldn't stop thinking about spending an evening with him. He had a draw on her; Santino was a magnetic force she couldn't fight.

She wandered down to the housekeeping department and rushed to the lockers to change out of her uniform, praying her supervisor wouldn't see her.

"Skating out of work?" a voice behind her asked.

She let out a breath of relief when she realized it was her friend Wendy. "It's, um, yeah," was all Clara could manage to say.

"The Slave Driver has been bitching about it for the last hour, but ignore her. I think it's romantic—like that movie *Pretty Woman*."

"He wasn't her boss in *Pretty Woman*, and I'm not dating Mr. Marchetti."

"Oh, so then you're just going home now or what? Do you want to catch a movie tonight then?"

"Uh, thanks, I have a thing to do...raincheck?" Clara brushed past her friend, hoping to avoid the scrutiny dinner with Santino would bring.

Back in her jeans and Converse sneakers, Clara was ten minutes into a Wheel of Fortune slot machine when her phone buzzed with a text. She glanced at it—it was from her stepfather, once again talking about the "moneybags boss" that paid his bail, except for now she realized he meant his new boss, not hers. She smiled as she slid her phone back into her jeans pocket.

She'd been playing for thirty minutes when her phone rang with a rare call. In her circles, no one ever called without first texting to warn her they were going to actually call. The number was local but she didn't recognize it, so she swiped to answer and said a quick prayer that it wasn't a bill collector.

"Sweet Clara, it's Santino. I apologize that this meeting is taking longer than I anticipated."

The sound of his voice made her feel warm inside. "Oh, it's fine. I'm playing slots—I never get to gamble."

"Spoken like a true local," he answered.

"It's not that so much, I just never have the extra cash. This is fun—I'm not worried about losing. Thanks for letting me play."

"Enjoy the casino and I promise to hurry. I'm quite excited to be alone with you tonight, Miss Denton." He hung up without a goodbye. Clara felt giddy adding his number to her contacts. *He called her!* Which meant he took the time to look up her number.

Santino set his mobile phone down and unmuted his conference call with Macau—the corporation was planning to expand there next year. But his mind wasn't on business, or on the massive profit projections his financial advisor was gushing over—his mind was on getting Clara Denton alone in his penthouse.

His best friend and second in command, Nicco Orsini sat across from him at the long conference table. Santino slid a note to him: "Go check on the girl. Don't let her leave."

Clara was in a state of euphoria—she was up five hundred dollars, and even though she knew the player's card she was gambling with had no cash value, the thrill of winning, along with the idea of dinner with Santino, had her happier than she'd been in a very long time. The cocktail waitress had even brought her a beer—the good stuff, not the watered down cheap stuff she usually ordered.

Her good luck dissipated when someone tapped her on the shoulder. She turned to see a tall woman, taller than she knew women could be, in a dour dark suit looking down at her. *Seriously,* she thought, *a pit boss worried over the slot machines?*

"Miss, where did you get that VIP card?" The woman stared at her as if she were a criminal.

"Um, Mr. Marchetti gave it to me," she answered. "Or lent it, let me use it, I guess."

"Mr. Marchetti?" the woman repeated with a snort.

The pit boss reached for the card and yanked it from Clara. "A card was stolen from a whale's guest in one of the guest suites just this morning. Would you know anything about that?"

"Oh, no, but um, this card I just got from his receptionist."

"His—meaning Santino Marchetti, the owner of this establishment?"

"Yeah, Santino. Go ask him."

The woman turned the card over in her hands before returning her glare to Clara. "Miss, this is a nice place, we don't need—"

"I know it's nice, I work here. If you'd take two seconds to check with—"

"You work here? In which department?"

"I'm a maid," Clara answered.

"Isn't that a coincidence—I think we now know who stole the VIP card from Mr. Morimoto's niece."

"Who is...huh?" Clara was confused and angry.

"Mr. Morimoto gambles in excess of ten million dollars a year at the Roman. That VIP card was stolen from his niece's room this very morning."

"Not *this* card," a voice said from behind them.

They both turned to look at him. He wore a brown suit with a teal tie, and when his eyes met Clara's, he smiled. *Nice to meet you finally,* he said to her. Although, he didn't say it; it just somehow appeared in her head as a thought. The sensation was so real she opened her mouth to answer and then stopped, her mouth slightly open as she struggled to stop staring into his eyes. They were unique—one was pale blue, like Santino's, but the other was a warm brown.

"Mr. Orsini," the pit boss stammered, "I'm sorry that this minor incident has drawn your attention."

"Sharon, this valued member of our staff is a guest of Santino's today—let's make her feel a little more welcome." He smiled wide at the furious pit boss—his white teeth gleaming under the casino lights.

"Yes, sir," she forced herself to say. "I apologize for the misunderstanding."

"That will be all, Sharon," Nicco said with a warm smile.

She turned on her heel and power walked away from them. When she was gone, Nicco turned to Clara again. "I'm Nicco. Santino is stuck on that call for a little while longer—I thought I might steal you for a drink?"

She nodded and took his hand as he led her toward the bar.

Nicco hoped to read the girl's mind, but was able to get very little from her. He ordered them a second round of drinks, hoping the alcohol would help. He'd tried from afar many times at Santino's insistence and had gotten very little, but he hoped being this close it would be easier.

"May I call you Clara?"

She nodded. "I heard you had quite a fright the other day in one of our rooms. I'm sorry about that," he said, again trying to search her mind for a trace of how she felt about the dead body she'd seen. There was nothing.

"Oh that, yeah, it was kind of crazy for a while, but Santino explained all that. He's been great to me." She took a sip of her beer—more of the good stuff; Nicco had ordered them Peronis.

"No matter what happens, I want you to know he's a good guy. He's saved me, more than once. Just always remember that, Clara."

She took another long sip. *What exactly is this guy trying to warn me about?*

"You work for him then, right? I mean, you're in charge here right after Santino?"

Nicco nodded.

"So you're my boss, too," she said.

He nodded again. "For now."

He signaled to the bartender that they were leaving, and stood to help Clara from her barstool. "It seems our friend is ready for you."

"Oh," Clara said. "Cool. Thanks for the drinks." *How did he know Santino was ready? He didn't look at a phone or anything,* she wondered.

It was sunset when Nicco escorted her onto Santino's terrace. In one corner, there was a spa tub and a small plunge pool. On the other side, an iron table was covered by a white tablecloth and set for dinner. Everywhere around her were flowers and candles. Santino stood at the rail, waiting for her, still dressed in his dark suit.

"Clara, I'm so glad you agreed to have dinner with me." He took her hands in his and signaled for Nicco to go.

"This is like a date on *The Bachelor!*"

"*The Bachelor?*"

"You know, the TV show. I was addicted to it when we had cable."

"I confess I watch very little television."

Santino signaled through the glass French doors to a waiter in the kitchen that they were ready to begin. Pulling a chair out at the table, he said, "Please, lovely Clara, do sit. You can continue to enlighten me on this fine television program as we dine, if that would suit you?"

When salad was served and the wine was poured, Clara looked down at the row of utensils next to her plate. She looked up to Santino, who was waiting for her to begin. "Oh crud, I can't remember how to do it. I know to start from the left and work in to the right?"

He was puzzled. "As far as...?"

She blushed. "I can't remember which fork to use, or what to do with these little ones on top."

He smiled—always an odd sensation for him, but she made him feel lighter and somehow freer when she was near. "I'll tell you a secret, my darling," he said, leaning in toward her. "No one at this table cares. Pick any utensil you'd like." She smiled wide at him.

She giggled and grabbed her dinner fork. "I'm going to use the big one."

He nodded to her, reaching for his own dinner fork and stabbing a cherry tomato with it. "And I am sure you will use it beautifully," he flirted.

Santino watched her eat—he loved the way she was always a little hungry. Hunger for food was a sensation he hadn't felt since he was human, and even then only the one time, during the dark period just prior to his being made eternal. His hunger now, the one that howled inside him every minute, was an insatiable lust for blood.

"Do you drink any white wine?" she said, jolting him back to the present. "I had a good one the other night at the bar. It was sweet."

He remembered the night at his bar—he'd watched her every move. She'd been sipping on a cheap riesling in between bottles of beer.

"I tend to prefer things red, but perhaps we should explore some fine whites together?"

The main course was served, and the waiter hastily plopped down an additional setting of dinner forks. Santino looked to Clara and nodded toward her place setting—causing her to giggle and reach for her dessert fork. "Well played," he teased as the waiter made a sharp turn to leave.

"So tell me about this *Bachelor* program that my terrace reminded you of," he said as he picked up his steak knife.

"Oh, well, it's basically one guy and a bunch of women and they go on dates and stuff and he eventually ends up with one."

"And this is entertaining?" He sliced into his steak, so rare that it was no longer warm even on the outside. Her eyes widened as the red fluid flowed from it. "I assure you yours is medium-rare."

She nodded and cut into her own filet mignon—relieved that it was far less bloody. "So yeah, it's a good show, but they go out on these fantasy one-on-one dates toward the end, and they are off the hook."

"My terrace is 'off the hook'?"

She laughed and looked around. "Yeah, in my world it kinda is."

"Well, then I'm honored to be your bachelor for the evening, Miss Denton."

She poked at her asparagus as she decided to ask the question that had been nagging at her. "Are you? I mean, a bachelor?"

He looked up at her, knife in his right hand. "I am."

"Have you ever been married?"

"Once," he answered.

"Divorced?"

"Annulled actually."

She poked at her steak, puzzled. Finally he set down his knife and fork and leaned forward to explain. "I'm from a very strict Catholic family—divorce was not an option. But it all worked out, we are still quite close."

"Your ex-wife?"

He nodded, hoping this line of conversation would end. "So, Clara, what happens on these fantasy dates you were telling me about? How do they conclude?"

The waiter set down their dessert and poured coffee, and when he left she felt her face grow warm as she answered his question. "Uh, they either go to separate rooms if they don't gel that much, or if they are into each other they share this over the top fantasy suite for the night."

His eyes sparkled as he watched her inhale her dessert.

When they were finished, he reached a hand for her and walked her to the edge of the terrace. She looked out over the glittering lights of the Strip down below. "It's so beautiful here," she said, leaning into him.

"I find you far more stunning than any view, Clara." His lips brushed against the back of her head. He loved the way she smelled.

She turned to face him, his lips inches from hers. "Why?"

"Why?" His fingers brushed across her chin—he loved the delicate lines of her face.

"Why is a guy like you into me? I don't get it."

His arms wrapped around her, pulling her body against his. Her eyes fluttered closed as he kissed her for the first time. The jolt when his skin touched hers gave way to a warm flush as the kiss deepened. When he pulled back, his forehead against hers, she sighed. "Wow, that was...just wow," was all she could manage to say.

"Well, Miss Denton, I suppose from here I can either drive you home, or perhaps you'd like to at least see the fantasy suite?"

She grinned, laying her head on his shoulder as he held her tight. "I don't want to leave," she whispered into his ear.

He lifted her from the floor and walked to his bedroom. As he sat her on the edge of his bed, she looked around. Candles flickered everywhere as she said, "You planned this."

"I hoped, nothing more."

He knelt in front of her on the floor, and she reached out to pull his tie off. She'd only seen him fully dressed, and she couldn't wait to finally see what was under the suit. As she unbuttoned his shirt, he leaned in to kiss her.

Clara ran her palms across his strong chest, pausing to feel his heart beat as they kissed. "See I do have heart," he whispered in her ear.

"May I?" he asked, pulling her t-shirt over her head. He needed to see her neck.

He loved her delicateness—the gentle lines of her collarbone, of her small breasts cradled in the simple cotton bra, but most of all, of her neck. Clara's neck drove him to delirium—it was long, and her pale skin showed every vein; every vein that carried her sweet blood so close to the surface of her skin.

"You are beautiful," he said as his lips skimmed across her neck, pausing to nibble her earlobe, and then back down, across the thumping artery, and down to her collarbone. He paused to smell her—beyond the faint hint of some cheap bodywash, she smelled warmly human. Santino, even during this short time, had grown to love the smell of Clara.

His tongue went lower, toying with the swelling flesh heaving over her small bra. He was going so slowly, and Clara wanted him—now. But as she reached to open her own bra, he stopped her. "Please darling, let me unwrap you. We'll never have a first time again."

She nodded. He leaned back to take his shirt off—the sight of his muscled torso made her feel as if she was going to pass out. Her hands wrapped around his back, desperate for him.

His sharp teeth toyed with the delicate side of her neck as he unhooked her bra and let it fall. With just the lightest touch from his fingertips, he stroked across a breast, down toward her pink nipples, rigid and yearning to be touched.

When his lips wrapped around one of them, she felt her hips thrust up—she'd never been teased like this. The few guys she'd slept with were always in a hurry, but Santino had taken longer to take her bra off than all of her other sexual encounters.

In desperation from the strong suction on her nipple, she reached for his waistband, pulling at the belt that kept her from what she wanted the most. "Lie back" he commanded, sensing she was on the edge before he'd even touched her below the waist.

When her head rested on the mattress, he pulled off her shorts. As his fingertip poked her swollen wetness through the cotton panties, he couldn't help but smile at them. There wasn't much whimsy in his life, and Clara's panties were a welcome change to the seriousness with which he lived.

"It's not Saturday," he said before running his tongue along the ridge of her sex beneath the thin undergarment.

"Uh, what?" she panted. She couldn't think about anything other than getting him inside her soon.

"These say Saturday, Miss Denton." His tongue once again poked at her through the cotton.

"They were clean—I didn't expect anyone to see them."

"Well, I am glad someone did see them." He pulled them from her and tucked them in the pocket of his suit pants—he needed to keep them.

Her hips once again rose from the bed as his tongue stroked her from one end to the other, driving her to a slow climax that left her shaking.

"Very sweet, my angel, very sweet," he said as his tongue swiped across his lips to savor the last of her.

She was still thrashing when his lips found hers again. Her tongue stroked his, the taste of her own climax surprising her. "Please," she begged into his mouth, pulling him closer.

"Please what, Clara? I won't go any further until you are begging me to, until you can't continue for one more second without me inside of you."

"Please make love to me, please fuck me, please..."

She bit her own lip hard enough to cause it to bleed as she heard the rip of a condom packet. Her legs wrapped around his powerful back as his mouth found hers. When his almost unbearable thickness spread her open and plunged deep, she howled as another orgasm ripped through her. Her pleasure was so mind-bending that she never noticed Santino licking the blood from the lip she'd bit.

As she fell asleep, wrapped around him, Santino could still taste her blood and her sweetness. He rarely enjoyed the same woman twice, but as he lay there intertwined with her, he knew he had to have more of Clara, and that emotion terrified him.

* * * * *

The next morning, the smell of coffee stirred her from sleep, the best sleep she'd had in months. Clara worried it had all been a wonderful dream, but he was there next to her, in his luxurious bed.

"Good morning my angel," he said. She reached for the white china mug of coffee he handed her.

She felt awkward, naked, and unsure of what to say. "Did you sleep okay?"

"I admit I'm not used to having anyone in my bed, but I could get used to seeing you here as the sun rises," Santino said with a kiss to the top of her hand.

"Oh crap," she blurted out. "My car is in the employee lot—we're not supposed to park there after our shifts."

"I think you'll be okay," he answered with a wink. "Oh, and Clara, I'm really sorry about the thing the other day; the security staff behaved poorly. I don't regret any of it though, because I'm delighted that I've gotten to know you."

"In a biblical sense?" she joked.

He reached for her hand again. "In *every* sense."

The phone on his nightstand buzzed, and Santino reached for it, glancing at a text. "I have to go downstairs and tend to an issue that just arose. Please stay, though. I'll send up breakfast."

She sipped her hot coffee, her stomach rumbling at the word breakfast. "Okay, for a little while. Is it alright if I take a shower?"

He nodded, relieved to not have to part with her just yet. "Of course. I believe there are some ladies' items in the guest room across the hall."

"You have a lot of women guests?" she asked with a raised eyebrow.

"My mother, I fear. She's a handful." Santino leaned in and kissed her before peeling the sheet back and walking toward his changing room—Clara's pulse raced at the sight of his perfect form naked again.

* * * * *

She decided to use the guest bathroom, and searched the dresser for a robe. When she unfolded the long terry cloth robe, a shirt fell out. She reached for it—it was covered in a giant red stain. The soiled garment seemed out of character in Santino's meticulous home, but she shoved it back where she found it and robe in hand, wandered into the guest room shower.

After a hot shower she dressed in the clothes she'd worn the night before, minus the panties she couldn't seem to find. A breakfast tray was waiting for her at Santino's dining room table as she emerged from the guest room, and she sat down with a second cup of coffee. Rarely did she have the luxury of breakfast, and when she did, it was usually cereal from the box—neither she nor Landon ever seemed to remember to buy milk.

As she chewed on a delicious sourdough roll, she glanced at a leather book across the mahogany table. On top of it sat an old fashioned pen—the kind that flowed ink. She knew she shouldn't, but reached for it.

The script was old-fashioned, and the first several pages were in Italian, but it seemed to be a journal. She'd noticed the night before that Santino's right index finger was ink-stained. Clara nearly choked on her bread when she read the first page written in English.

> *"Blood will have blood," sayeth the poet. I will have her blood, and its sweetness will sustain me.*

Clara stared at the words, a chill running down her spine. She thought back to the body she'd seen, the one Santino had convinced her was a mannequin. *It was so real!* But Clara had been to those Cirque de Soleil shows twice, and the effects were better than any Hollywood movie—she didn't know what to believe. Or whom.

She glanced at her phone—there was nothing from the man she'd just spent the night with, but there was a text from Landon, teasing her about hooking up with her boss, and another from that strange blogger guy Matthew Hunter. He wanted to have lunch with her, and swore he had proof that her boss wasn't who she thought he was. Unable to quell her curiosity, she decided to see the odd blond again.

Meet me at Tommy Rocker's tomorrow @11. But not because I believe you, only because I want a burger.

Matthew replied with simply an emoji of a burger and a thumbs up.

* * * * *

Clara was frantic as she wove through stop and go traffic toward downtown. She was late, as usual, but traffic was light that day and she made it to the Flamingo Drug and Alcohol Abuse Center with five minutes to spare. Visiting hours started at ten, her father had said.

"Hey, baby," he said when he saw her walk into the lobby.

She hugged him and handed him a small package. "Give it to her," she said to his confused eyebrow raise.

"Aw, that's sweet of you Clara, and I'm so geeked that you're here, but bad news," he said, glancing toward the stern receptionist.

"Bad news?"

"Well, it seems Amanda lost her visitation today."

Clara glared at him. She was tired of her mother's constant self-sabotage. "For doing what?" she hissed.

"An aspirin—she had a headache and instead of going to the nurse, she snuck one from another resident." He chuckled as he said, as if the offense were so silly it required a laugh. But Clara was not amused.

"She broke the rules—and I came all this way and now I can't see her! How dare she do this to me."

"To *you*," he said with the shake of his head. "She screwed up, but this isn't like a mortal sin. She's been clean this whole time."

"It's her birthday, though," Clara said as she looked at the small gift-wrapped box her father held in his hands. She'd spent all morning going from store to store until she finally found the butterfly pendant that her father had been arrested for stealing. *Ten dollars,* she'd thought as she paid for it, *he went to jail for ten dollars.*

"Can you give me a ride back?" he asked. "I had Jimmy drop me, but don't have a ride home."

She nodded, feeling defeated. "Let me give my boss a quick call," she said as she pulled her phone from her pocket.

"Miss, no cell phone use in here," the receptionist snapped, pointing to the sign of rules.

In the parking lot, she called Santino. "I'm so mad—she screwed up and now we can't see her."

"I'm so sorry, my angel. I'd love to pull some strings and make that visit happen. It's her birthday, correct?"

"Strings? You can pull strings here?" Her mood suddenly lightened.

"Well, of course I could, but that might be construed as trying to rescue you again, and I'd hate for that to come between us as we're getting so close."

"Oh," she said. "Close?"

"Close."

"How close?" she flirted.

"I'll call you tonight and we can discuss it."

"It's a deal. And Santino, please pull the strings. Help isn't rescue, I get that now, and I really need your help."

"Done. Give me five minutes." He hung up without a goodbye.

She went back into the rehab center. "In the box, it's the necklace isn't it?" he asked holding it up.

She sat next to him in a green vinyl chair. "Yes. And I got her a bottle of perfume from me—that musk she loves."

They sat there in silence until he finally said, "I guess we should go. Maybe you could call her later?"

She nodded, but didn't move from her seat. The phone rang behind the counter, and the receptionist was arguing with the caller. "Fine," she eventually snapped and slammed down the receiver.

Looking over at them, she waved her hand toward the secured door. "Looks like she's been cleared to have visitors."

"Because it's her birthday I bet," Clara said with a wink.

The receptionist sneered at her. "Or because your boss called the Director with a massive donation if she would make an exception for your mother."

"Coolio," Clara said. "I must be a great employee."

Her father grabbed her hand and jumped up. "Kick ass! Let's go see her before they change their minds, baby," he urged as the door buzzed open.

SIX

It was early evening when she heard from Santino again.

"My sweet angel, how was your visit with your mother?"

"It was okay. She still blames everyone else for her problems. Thank you so much for doing that though—it meant the world to my dad."

"You are more than welcome. Clara, I'm sorry I had to go this morning. Business complication, I'm afraid. I'd love to make it up to you."

She couldn't answer for a moment, and finally said, "You already have, plus I even got breakfast out of it." She smiled—she wanted to flirt but wasn't sure how.

"The Harvest Bakery at the Roman is the best in town. I hope you enjoyed it."

"The sourdough is heavenly!" Clara didn't want to spend her phone call with Santino discussing bread, but she desperately wanted to keep him on the line.

"They bring in the dough from San Francisco twice a week, so it's authentic."

"I've always wanted to go to San Francisco," Clara said. She'd never been farther than Salt Lake City, and had only flown a handful of times.

"Let's go then," Santino said. "It's supposed to be sweltering in the Valley this weekend, I wouldn't mind escaping to somewhere cooler."

"What?" Clara was confused—had he just asked her to go away with him?

"Clara Marie Denton, will you join me tomorrow for an overnight in the city by the Bay? I'll spoil you, I promise."

The butterflies stirred in her stomach once again. A voice in her head told her it wasn't wise, but her heart leapt at the prospect of another night with Santino.

"Um, that sounds like a blast, but I have to work tomorrow afternoon. Can we hang out Sunday though?" She cringed as she heard herself—she sounded so immature compared to Santino.

"I'll pick you up at ten. I can't wait to show you the city for the first time."

"Santino, I can't just ditch my job." She thought of her supervisor, and the shit she'd get from the rest of housekeeping if they found out she'd slept with the boss.

"You're not *ditching*, my darling. You are accompanying your boss on a fact-finding trip. We'll check out the finest hotel suite in San Francisco and see how it compares to our own lovely guest rooms. We might have to spend a lot of time in bed to truly gather the facts." She could hear the flirt in his voice—and the desire for her. It still seemed too good to be true.

* * * * *

Clara was at the rickety kitchen table when Landon came home from work later that evening. "I brought chicken Alfredo, Clara Belle. Tons of it—a big party ordered it then decided it was too garlicky. We'll be eating this heart attack on a plate for the next week."

She looked up at him. "There's no such thing as too much garlic!"

"Well said, baby girl. Let's nosh!"

He grinned at her through his braces—she loved Landon. They'd met their senior year in high school and were instant friends. Clara was the shy, studious girl with few friends, but everyone loved Landon. He was always the class clown, and as a self-proclaimed bisexual, the curiosity alone was enough to keep him popular. Without him, she'd never have survived her first semester at UNLV.

As Landon heated the discarded pasta in the microwave, Clara dug through a cabinet until she found a bottle of cheap merlot. "Santino would know the perfect wine pairing, and this wouldn't be it," she joked.

"You spent the night with him, huh? You have that glow," Landon said with a wink.

"Yes, it was incredible. But he's, I don't know Landon he's different." She filled their tumblers with wine as he dumped heaps of the greasy white pasta dish on their plates.

"Different good or different bad?" Landon asked as they sat at the table.

"I'm not sure, both maybe. He asked me to go to San Fran with him tomorrow." Her mind wandered to the stained shirt she'd found and to his writings, and she decided not to tell Landon, although she couldn't exactly place why.

"Overnight? He's paying, right?"

"Yeah, but...I just met him. And, he's my boss and everything."

"Damn, Clara Belle, live a little. If you're really worried tell him you need to bring a chaperone—maybe we can have a three-way."

Clara shook her head at him. "I'm not sure what to pack."

"Let's go grab you some new threads—you still have some money left from Mr. Dark and Dreamy?"

"I still feel bad about cashing that check, but yeah. Let's shop then—Target is open until eleven."

"Target? You cannot date Mr. Rich and Delicious in Target clothes, baby girl."

"I'm not spending all of that money—and I love Target. You drive though, I'm out of gas."

* * * * *

Clara woke early the next morning, agonizing over what to wear. She'd spent over a hundred dollars at Target the night prior, and managed to get a dress, a pair of heels, jeans, and at Landon's insistence, a sexy red lingerie set that she couldn't look at without blushing.

In her broken mirror, she struggled to get ready. Her hair wouldn't behave—no matter how much body she tried to give it, it just fell flat around her shoulders. "What does he even see in you!" she howled at her image in the cracked mirror.

At exactly ten, there was a knock at the door. Santino stood there—his white teeth gleaming in a wide grin. It took her a second to process him—she'd only ever known him to be dressed in tailored suits, but that morning he stood at her sun-faded door in jeans—sexy jeans. He seemed younger in casual clothes, and she realized she didn't even know how old he was.

"You look beautiful," he said, leaning in to kiss her. "Shall we?"

"Can I tell my roommate where we'll be? He gets protective," she lied.

Santino stared at her for a second, hoping he could read her thoughts, but nothing came to him. He did sense her caution, and was annoyed at her distrust in him after the special night they'd shared.

"Certainly. However, it is a surprise. You can notify Mr. Miller of your whereabouts when we arrive."

"How do you know his name?"

He didn't answer. Picking up her battered duffle bag, he crooked one arm to her and walked her down the concrete stairs to the dark car waiting at the curb.

In the back of the car, Clara stared at her phone—could she be tracked if he drove her out into the desert? She'd known Santino for such a short time, and there were so many red flags in her mind. At the same time, she knew she was far too into him to walk away. He reached for her phone and slid it in his back pocket. "Mobile phones are a blessing and a curse. Let's focus on one another today, Clara."

She nervously nodded. "This isn't the way to the airport," she said, looking through the tinted windows as the city passed by. Glancing at his ink-stained fingers, her mind went back to the words she'd seen written in an old-fashioned script that she knew had to be Santino's.

"Blood will have blood," sayeth the poet. I will have her blood, and its sweetness will sustain me.

The words were vaguely familiar, and she searched her mind for any connection with the Blood Lust Killer, but couldn't think of anything to tie the two together. Santino reached for her, his fingers cradling her chin, forcing her to look into his eyes. "Trust me, Clara."

She was relieved when the long car pulled into Henderson Executive—the smaller airport that mostly served private jets and the helicopters tourists took to the Grand Canyon. A gleaming white jet sat just outside the hangar, and the words Eternal Enterprises were written on both the jet and the side of the hangar in maroon. Her paycheck came from Eternal Enterprises.

Santino took her hand and led her from the car to the plane as the driver handed their bags over to one of the two pilots. Once they were settled into side-by-side leather seats, Santino leaned in toward Clara. He longed to smell her, to catch a whiff of her blood, but the only smell he could catch repulsed him.

"It's a short flight, no time to use the bedroom in the back," Santino said once they were airborne, his hand resting on her thigh. Clara blushed; she was nervous, but couldn't wait to have his hands on her body again.

She was confused when he pulled a packet of gum from his jeans pocket. It wasn't an offer, she realized, it was a demand. She unwrapped the cinnamon gum and popped it into her mouth, embarrassed at the suggestion that her breath was bad.

"It is the garlic, my darling, that's all. I have an odd aversion to the scent of it. Please don't be offended." His arm wrapped around her, pulling her toward him. He inhaled again, and finally got the satisfaction he was seeking—he could smell the beautiful mortal, her sweetness taunting him, the scent of her blood the ultimate aphrodisiac.

"I should have thought of that, sorry. I had leftover chicken Alfredo for breakfast. Aren't you from Italy? Don't they have that there?"

"Rome, yes, however I don't believe I've ever seen *that* on a menu there."

After two glasses of champagne, Santino excused himself to the lavatory in the rear of the plane. As soon as he'd latched the door, he pulled Clara's buzzing phone from his back pocket. It took his superior mind less than thirty seconds to figure out her lock code. The first two texts were innocuous—chit-chat from her perky roommate. What bothered him were the three phone calls and the two texts she'd received from the Hunter. He fought to control his rage at the thought of the complications Matthew Hunter presented to his plans for Clara.

The first text was bad enough:

Are we still meeting for lunch? The Tommy Rocker's on Dean Martin right? We need to talk.

But the second one made even his cold skin grow hot:

Clara where are you? Don't stand me up—#ffs he's a vampire! Oh and a SERIAL KILLER!!

"Goodbye, Hunter," Santino said out loud as he deleted the texts, two voicemails, and all of the recent calls from Matthew. To ensure no further complications that weekend, he also blocked the Hunter's number from her phone.

When he emerged, she was smiling at him. When she smiled, his dark world lit up. This young woman touched him like no one ever had before, mortal or eternal. "Let me show you the world," he said as he fell into the seat next to her.

"Start with San Francisco?"

"Sure thing," he said, reaching for her. He needed to hold her—her presence soothed him. "You probably don't like chocolate, but if you did..." he teased.

"Chocolate! Feed me chocolate and I'm yours forever," she flirted. Clara was on her third glass of champagne, and she felt bold. "Oh, give me my phone, please, I want to show Landon the jet—he'll never believe it."

Santino kissed her hand. "Not in the air, I'm afraid, it's against the rules. We'll get some pictures on the way home before we take off."

"Deal," she said.

* * * * *

"Are you hungry, my angel?" Santino asked as soon as they were settled into the waiting car.

"Starving," she said, looking out the window, searching for signs of the city.

"Well, that would be an exaggeration. However, I did promise you the best lunch in San Francisco, did I not?"

"Oh, are we dressed okay?" She glanced down at her new jeans, relieved he wasn't in a suit this time. "I have a dress in my bag, I can change."

"You'll be fine," he said with a wink.

Santino leaned forward to talk to their driver. "Drop us at Fisherman's Wharf, Mario. I'll text you when we're ready to head to the hotel."

Santino held her hand as they walked down the tourist-clogged Fisherman's Wharf. Her hair blew behind her in the wind as her wide-eyes took it all in. When she smiled at him and squeezed his hand, he was sure she was the most exquisite being he'd ever seen. He had to protect her no matter what the cost. She couldn't end up like the rest.

"Where's the restaurant?" she asked as they walked.

"My girl is hungry as usual," he teased. "It's more of a stand than a restaurant, but this place has the best chowder on the West Coast."

She expected to be wined and dined by Santino, but the sight of him carrying two giant bread bowls with white soup sloshing from the top was far more romantic than any five-star restaurant.

Clara hovered over the seating area in the packed restaurant as Santino ordered, and was lucky enough to grab a tiny table that she wiped down herself. She grinned as he set the plastic tray and two Coronas on the beat-up metal table. "I promise I'll class it up tonight, if you'd like, but I couldn't bring you to San Francisco without feeding you authentic clam chowder in a sourdough bread bowl."

"Do you come here often? To San Francisco?" she asked as she dipped a chunk of the bread into the creamy soup.

He debated how to answer, but settled on the truth. "I lived here once, long ago."

"After you came from Rome? You don't really have an Italian accent, but you were raised there right?"

He nodded. "It's been ages since I lived in Rome, but my family still maintains a home there."

"Oh, so you lived here before you moved to Vegas?"

He took a long sip from his bottle of beer. "Yes, and New Orleans prior to that," he answered.

"You move a lot, wow. I've always lived in Vegas. As a kid I dreamed of living somewhere where there was snow—I was convinced that Santa was better to kids in snowy places. I know it's dumb."

"There's nothing *dumb* about Santa Claus, my dear, he's quite an interesting guy," he said with a smile. "Well, I mean except for that thing about stealing the souls of bad children."

She laughed and nudged him with her foot. "You can be funny, you know, for such a serious dude."

"I *was* being serious!" He raised an eyebrow at her. "But eat up, my angel, because I have another surprise in store for dessert."

* * * * *

"Do you think the murderer has stopped?" she blurted out as she unwrapped a square of chocolate. They'd just left the Ghirardelli Chocolate factory with a ridiculous haul of the iconic wrapped squares they were famous for. Santino insisted Clara have every possible variety, and he bought extra for her to take to her roommate. He loved seeing her giddy over the chocolate, but he did *not* want to discuss the Vegas killings.

When Santino didn't want to answer a question, he ignored it. No one in his world would ever dare to press him on it. But Clara wasn't from his world. "Well," she pressed, "what do you think? Will the killer strike again?"

He stopped and turned toward her. "So wise so young, they say do never live long."

"Shakespeare," she said. "But that doesn't answer my question."

He pulled her close to him, leaning in to kiss her. He could taste the chocolate on her lips; he could hear the blood in her veins crying out to him. *I need to have her soon,* he thought.

"Okay, I'll drop it," she said as his lips left hers.

"Clara, I believe the monster that is hunting the women of Las Vegas will continue to inflict horror until the howling need within him is satisfied or he is destroyed, whichever comes first."

"Fair enough," she said as they began to walk hand in hand toward the waiting car. "Was that quote from *King Lear*?"

"*Richard the Third*."

"He'd be a crazy dude to hang out with right? Shakespeare, I mean, not Richard."

"He is," Santino said flatly as the driver opened the car door for them. "But Richard was before my time," he added as he climbed into the backseat next to her. *If she only knew,* he thought.

"Last fall the library at school had a First Folio from 1623 on display—it was the closest I've ever been to something that old." Santino thought about his friend Will, still wandering the banks of the Thames in a half-dead state, haunting the players who performed his works throughout the ages.

"So you like old things? Older men, maybe?" He reached for her hand and cradled it in his.

She squeezed his hand. "Hm, how much older? You've never said."

"A month or two," he said with a squeeze of her hand. "Mario, can you stop over at the bridge? I'd like to walk Miss Denton across it. After that, I think we'll visit the rare books store on Geary before we head to the hotel."

Halfway across the iconic Golden Gate Bridge, Clara stopped to look over the railing. Santino moved behind her, his hands on the railing fencing her in. Her silky hair was whipped back by the wind as she pointed to a small island in the Bay. "Look, it's Alcatraz! It looks so much smaller than I expected."

"And closer," he said, leaning in to smell her hair. Santino loved that Clara didn't wear a lot of perfume—she usually simply smelled of soap and some cheap shampoo. Her blood as it coursed through her thin veins was usually the scent he was after, but that afternoon, he was content with his nose buried in her hair.

"It's so incredible. Can we go see it?"

"Perhaps tomorrow. The last ferry has already departed, unless you're a strong swimmer, that is."

"I've heard it's shark infested," she said, scanning the water below.

"Indeed. The scariest form of the undead in existence."

"Huh? Oh, yeah, sharks. I think that's just the Great White that lives so long though."

He leaned in again, wishing he could protect her from all danger—but the nagging voice inside him knew that he *was* the danger.

"Thank you for bringing me here," she said, turning around to face him. He leaned in, his lips inches from hers.

"You are quite welcome. I love walking the bridge, but I can't wait to get you back to the hotel."

"I've been thinking about it all day," she confessed, wrapping her arms around his waist. His lips met hers, gently at first, then harder, needier. Despite the nagging voice in his head telling him he was already getting too close to this human, caring more than he should, her lips parted wider, her tongue begging his to enter.

She pressed into his hardness, oblivious to the throngs of tourists brushing past them. It was he who regretfully pulled away from the kiss—he wanted her alone, and naked, as soon as possible.

"Well, I don't often make out in public on bridges, Miss Denton, clearly you are a corrupt influence on me," he teased with a wink. "Let's get to the hotel before we explore this situation in any greater detail."

As they neared the entrance of the bridge, it happened.

A ragged old woman, homeless Clara assumed, rushed at them, her crooked finger inches from Santino's face. "An abomination! Blood drinkers in the sunlight? It is forbidden." Clara looked around for help as the woman pushed her hands against Santino's chest. He didn't budge.

Santino answered her, but in another language. She'd taken French in high school, and she could pick out a few words, one of them being *sorcière*, which she remembered meant *witch*.

His hand touched her forearm, and the woman pulled away from him as if she'd been electrocuted. "You have forgotten your place, eternal Santino, you and all of those who walk with you. God will have you burn!"

Clara pulled at his hand. "Let's just go. She's crazy."

"Oh I'm crazy, am I, pretty girl? I know about you, little whore—you killed your father."

His eyes darkened as he addressed the old woman again in French.

The old woman shook for a second before backing away. Santino tugged at Clara, "Let's go, before I do something I'll regret."

The woman called out after them. "You have sparked with this being, eternal one, and she will be the cause of great suffering to you."

In the back of the dark car, Clara was nearly catatonic. Her whole body shook as Santino reached over and fastened her seatbelt.

"Mad ramblings of an old woman, my angel, please don't let it disturb you." He laid his hand on her thigh.

"What she said, it's just, I guess it hit a nerve." The tears rolled down her cheeks. "How did she know your name? And what did you say to her? You spoke to her in French. She knew your *name*—holy shit, what just happened?"

Santino took a deep breath. He needed to neutralize this situation quickly. Clara was far too smart for her own good. And yet, her intellect was the thing that drew him to her the most. *And* the spark—*that damn old hag knew,* he thought, unable to deny any longer that Clara wasn't just another girl.

"I'm sorry she upset you, angel. It's sad the level of mental illness among the homeless. She didn't say my name; she called me Satan. The accent made it sound that way—she's French Creole."

"Oh, I thought...I heard it wrong," Clara said, thinking back to what happened. The woman did have a strong accent; she probably did say Satan. "Well that was nasty of her."

"Accurate, I must admit. I am Satan," he teased.

"That's not funny," she said, relaxing as his hand moved up her leg.

"Don't let it bother you, my sweet angel. I'll cheer you up at the bookstore, I promise."

"Oh," was all she could think to say. "It's just what she said about my—about... well she just freaked me out, that's all."

"She said that you killed your father, to be precise." Santino studied her, the tears rolling down her cheeks again as his words hit. He tried to penetrate her mind, but it was locked up like a fortress.

"We don't have to talk about such things. Perhaps more chocolate will make it better?" He reached for the bag of Ghirardelli chocolates.

Clara had no intention of confiding in this man she barely knew, but when he pulled off the dark sunglasses and his eyes met hers, the words flowed out.

"The summer I turned nine, I watched my mother have an affair with our neighbor. Daddy would go to work, and the man would come over. In our living room, they'd get high and have sex—all while I was kept in my bedroom, sometimes for six to seven hours at a time."

Santino put down the square of chocolate in his hand and focused on her. As much as it pained him, he needed to know her secrets, her darkest places. It was the only leverage he had against his own demons. "Go on, Clara, you can tell me anything."

She brushed away the tears with the back of her hand. "One day, I had to pee so badly I couldn't hold it in any longer. But *he* was in the bathroom, and smacked me when I opened the door. When I told Mom, she yelled at me. I was mad, Santino, so mad that I did something I can never take back."

"Yes?" Santino studied her; she was about to bare her soul.

"I told my dad when he got home from work."

Santino tried again to look into her mind, but only caught little pieces of the story.

"Clara, you are not responsible for your parents' problems."

"It's worse. Oh my God, I've never told anyone but Landon this. Daddy did nothing—he said nothing, he went to work as usual, nothing changed. Until..."

"Until?"

"Until one day she went out for the day. Her friend Tillie took her to get their nails done at the mall. I'd been out riding my bike, but when I got home, he was hanging there."

Clara doubled over at the pain from remembering—at the agony of what she had done.

Santino's hand caressed her back. In that moment he wanted to shield her from all pain, to take her into his arms and never let go. "You don't have to talk about it, Clara, if you don't want to." *Damn the whole thing,* he thought, *I will not hurt her no matter what.*

She spoke again, her pained voice barely above a whisper. "He was hanging in the closet—blue, swollen, and..." She sobbed, her face in her hands at the memory that haunted her day and night. "I killed him, it was my fault, Mom even said so. 'He couldn't handle it, Clara, you did this' she said that day."

Santino wrapped around her, desperate to absorb her pain. "You didn't do it, Clara, it wasn't your fault." He took her chin in his hands and forced her to look into his eyes. "Darling, you were a child. He would have found out sooner or later, if he didn't already know. You did *not* do that to him."

She sniffled, unable to shake the guilt.

Before the driver opened their door, Santino turned to her. "I lost my father, too, my angel. And, I confess I also bear a lot of the burden of that."

Santino had the driver drop them off a few blocks from the bookstore. As they turned a corner, he took her in his arms. He needed to touch her, to feel her warm body against his cold one. Clara was more to him now than damage control or even attraction; with her, he felt emotions he hadn't felt in ages, if ever.

"'In black ink my love may still shine bright,'" he said in her ear.

Her eyes fell to his ink stained fingers. "Shakespeare," she answered as he held her, the swirl of the other pedestrians on the crowded city street maneuvering around them.

"Sonnet Sixty-Five. Perhaps we'll pick up a dusty old book of them and I'll read to you in the hotel."

"I'd love that." Nothing interested her more than old books.

"Naked in the tub would be best I think," he said with a tug on her hand. "There's a coffee shop next door, shall we grab a little caffeine jolt before we lose ourselves in literature?" He wrapped his arm around her as they walked along the crowded sidewalk.

Minutes later, they were seated at a small round table. Clara sipped a sugary caramel latte while poking at a giant frosted donut. Santino sipped a triple espresso as he watched her devour the sweet snack.

"You should watch the sugar, my angel. You're addicted to sweets."

"So you're my boss, but you can't tell me what to eat," she teased, dipping her index finger into the whipped cream and crammed it into her mouth. "Besides, you drink coffee like it's water. How are you not in a permanent state of buzz?"

"It doesn't have much of an effect on me. I just like the richness of it until it's an appropriate time to indulge in wine."

"Can we go? That red-headed chick over at the counter is making eyes at you." Clara glanced over his shoulder again at the woman. Ever since they'd sat down, she'd stared at Santino, and when he'd taken Clara's hand, the woman grimaced as if it pained her.

"So I'm attracting crazy people today?" He drank the final few sips of his espresso and turned to look, but the woman was gone.

* * * * *

It happened again at the bookstore. She kept looking at them over the shelves until Clara finally nudged Santino. "Did you see her? She's here now; the woman from the coffee shop. She's following us."

Santino looked up from the copy of *Justine* that he was thumbing through. "I don't know her," he said casually, his eyes drifting back to the pages.

"She's beautiful," Clara whispered, her eyes glued to the auburn-haired, green-eyed, fair skinned creature following them.

"Darling, I'm sure she is bewitching, but right now I only have eyes for you."

She smiled as he kissed her forehead. "When do we check in to the hotel?" she asked sheepishly.

"Well, I was trying to be a good host and not just take you to bed, but I'm all for the hotel, my angel." He nuzzled against her, the redheaded woman's eyes still on them.

"Forgive my boldness, but the journey to our lodgings might take a while in the traffic—do you need to visit the ladies' room first? All that coffee, I thought possibly?"

She nodded. Sometimes she swore he could read her mind—she'd just looked around for a restroom. "In the corner, over there," he gestured. "I'll text for our driver in the meantime."

When Clara was out of sight, he walked over to the witch who'd been trailing him for the last two hours.

"What do you want, Estrella?"

She licked her lips. "You, my blood thirsty Santino."

"Never," he said. "I don't lie with witches."

"Earlier today, my mother was rude to you. I wanted to apologize, to explain."

"She's lucky to still be walking the earth. This human means a lot to me, and that old hag upset her."

"I don't want trouble, Santino, we already have enough of that. My mother behaved improperly, thank you for granting her mercy."

"I haven't...yet. Now go, the mortal had better not see you again."

* * * * *

In the hotel suite, Santino knelt in front of Clara. He had to taste her again—immediately. Blood, wine, and the sweet fluid of women—those were his three favorite tastes.

His tongue had only enjoyed her once—but it was all he'd thought about since. She moaned as his nose pressed into her, teasing her through her clothing. Her legs nearly buckled as his fingers reached up to tug at the button on her jeans.

"I've missed you; I've missed this," he said as he let the jeans fall to the floor.

Her skin tingled as his lips pressed at her through her thin cotton panties. Only two others had attempted to pleasure her with their mouths, but not like Santino. Clara's last boyfriend would nervously swipe a few times, but lacked the patience to take her to ecstasy the way Santino had that one night they spent together—and he'd done it not once, not twice, but three times. And now, despite her embarrassment at her less than sexy panties that didn't match her bra, or the nagging words from Landon about how she should wax or shave, she needed his tongue inside her again.

"So ready, my angel," he moaned, the hardness in his jeans nearly painful. His agile fingers lowered the delicate panties, and his lips began with her feet, kissing their way up to her inner thigh. "You are so perfect," he whispered, his hands cradling her firm behind as his lips brushed against her.

Her legs braced as his tongue explored her— not hurried, or urgent, but slowly, savoring her as he would the finest wine in his collection.

"Santino, please," she begged as his tongue plunged into her again, teasing her, keeping her just on the edge.

"Patience, Clara, let it build." He leaned her back on the edge of the bed. One toe at a time, his skilled mouth had her thrashing on the bed—begging and pleading. In his younger years he was always good with women, and men if the mood struck him, but now, after hundreds of years of practice, Santino could make even the most frigid scream in ecstasy.

By the time his tongue stroked her throbbing clit, she'd been screaming his name for twenty minutes. By the time he entered her, hard and fast, she was so desperate for him that her teeth bit into his shoulder as her nails sank into his back.

Afterward, exhausted, they lay wrapped together in the sheets. Santino stroked Clara's leg as her fingertips danced across the angry red mark where she'd bit him. "I'm normally the one who does the biting, my darling," he teased as her eyes closed.

She was too tired to notice the bite mark heal beneath her fingers.

When she woke up, the sun was setting. She saw Santino standing on the small balcony of the suite, a cigarette dangling from his lips as he watched the sunset. She couldn't take her eyes off of him as the sun sank below the horizon. He snuffed the cigarette out and turned to the side, his face lit only by the full moon. She reached for her phone to snap a picture of him. Clara knew he didn't want to be photographed, but he was too beautiful, too perfect, in that light. She couldn't resist.

The click of her phone caused him to look at her. Her tummy fluttered as he walked toward her, naked in the moonlight. She expected him to reach for her phone, but he didn't. He smiled, and reached for her instead, his lips nibbling at hers as he entered her once again.

* * * * *

When Clara woke late the next morning, Santino was gone.

She wrapped the robe draped across the bed around her shoulders and walked into the living room of the suite. On the table, there was a handwritten note on the breakfast tray—and she noticed the breadbasket was overflowing with sourdough bread. It was on the hotel stationary, but he'd written it with his flowing ink pen, in his old-fashioned script.

"Mystery solved," she said as she picked up the note. "It's his writing."

My darling, please forgive my absence. I often find it hard to rest, especially as the golden sun kisses the horizon. The Pier is calling me, so I believe I will take the liberty of indulging in a sunrise walk as you slumber. I miss you already. – S

She smiled as she slathered the tangy sourdough toast with strawberry jam. It had been a magical weekend, and she couldn't wait to be in his arms again. She reached for her phone; Santino had left it sitting near the note. She was surprised Matthew hadn't called—she'd stood him up the day before in her haste to be with Santino. There were, however, several texts from Landon. She pressed his photo on her contact list to call him.

"Hey, Clara Belle!" He'd answered on the first ring.

"Well, I'm here with him! We came out on a private jet—his private jet."

"You have hit the ultimate sugar daddy, my girl. I'm completely jelly."

"Yesterday was the best day, and it ended in the perfect night. I just can't believe it's happening to *me*. What can a guy like that really see in me?"

Landon shoved a piece of peanut butter toast into his mouth, and in his normal garbled chew-talking said, "It's about time you started to see the truly kickass, beautiful woman that you are."

She was quiet for a moment, trying to absorb it all. "Is there any news on the murders?" she finally asked.

"No, word around the academy is maybe he's either left town or gone on a break. They do that, these serial types. This is the longest stretch between killings since he started. Hey, where is lover boy now?"

"He went for a walk. I'd better get in the shower—I'll see you tonight."

"Okay, later, but I want every gooey detail! Preferably with pictures."

* * * * *

Santino returned an hour later, and Clara breathed a sigh of relief. She'd convinced herself during her shower that he wanted to get away from her. But when he returned, his face lit up as he took her in his arms and guided her toward the bedroom.

"I missed you, I ached for you," he whispered in her ear at the bedroom doorway.

"How long do we have? I mean, when is checkout?" She glanced around at the disheveled bedroom—they needed to pack, it was nearly ten.

"We'll leave when we're ready—do you really live your life by checkout times, sweet angel?" He looked into her eyes—he could smell the sweetness of her blood just beneath the fresh scent of some perfume she'd applied.

"I haven't stayed in a hotel since our senior year trip to Tahoe," she confessed. "But I clean them all the time, and at the Roman, we generally like our guests to vacate by eleven."

"You are too bright, too special, to be cleaning hotel rooms. If you insist on working, when we get back let's find you a more suitable position in my organization."

"Santino, no, I can't do that."

"Do what?" He pulled her closer to the bed, the faint sound of the TV murmuring in the background.

"Get ahead by sleeping with the boss," Clara answered.

"That's not what I meant—although, I very much want you to continue to sleep with the boss." His lips found her neck, gliding to his favorite part—that area where the artery thumped blood against her nearly translucent skin. He had to bite his tongue, taste his own blood, in order to avoid nibbling her.

"Santino, look," she snapped suddenly, jolting him from his worship of her neck.

She reached for the remote and turned up the volume. The local news was on.

"Oh my God!" Clara said, her hand covering her mouth.

Santino glanced to the screen, unsure of what could be more important than his lips on her skin. "So? Someone was killed in San Francisco? You're a Vegas girl and you're shocked by a murder?"

"Santino, listen—the corpse found under the Bay Bridge was *drained of her blood.*"

He sat down on the bed, his head spinning. He pulled Clara into his lap, mostly so she wouldn't see his face, read his expression. *This is unfortunate,* he thought.

Clara was glued to the screen, but Santino didn't want to hear the details. It didn't matter. He buried his face into the back of her neck—he loved the fresh smell of her silky hair. His felt a jolt, however, as they showed a photo of the victim. His heart pounded against Clara's back—should he tell her?

"Clara," he began, but she hushed him.

"Listen, they just said she's an attorney from Las Vegas! I recognize her from those immigration attorney commercials."

He forced himself to look around her to look at the face on the screen again. It was a screenshot of her TV ad that ran constantly on Las Vegas channels. *Laura Hidalgo,* she said her name was in the commercial—but he barely remembered her name. Santino did remember her face, however, and the way her long black hair fanned out across the crisp white Italian linens that afternoon at the Roman. He never took women to his penthouse, so they'd instead used a vacant room at the hotel.

Clara's mind raced as the pieces clicked together. "Do you recognize her?" she asked, her heart pounding as the questions plagued her about the man she was falling in love with.

"Vaguely," he lied. She'd been less than a one-night stand—he'd spent less than an hour with the flirty attorney in his office before they'd fallen into bed together. She'd met with him that afternoon a little over a month ago to discuss legal services for an employee whose ill mother was facing deportation. He hadn't thought about her since, but now there she was, lying dead under a bridge because of him. The pattern had become undeniable.

"Please don't get angry, but I have to ask," Clara began, terrified that she was about to lose the man she barely had, but she had to know.

His lips found her neck again, his sharp canines hovering just over her carotid artery. "Ask, my sweet angel," he said in a near moan. He was finally about to taste her.

She took a deep breath. "This morning, please tell me you weren't near the Bay Bridge. I mean, it's just, after the thing at the Roman, I mean the police still have that on file somewhere I'm sure, and we just came from Vegas to here, she's from Vegas, I mean, I just want to work it out before we get back. I'm sorry, please don't hate me for asking."

Santino allowed his sharp teeth to graze across the thumping vein before he pulled away from her delicate throat. "No, I walked Pier 39. I stopped at the coffee house, too, that famous one." He tightened his grip around her waist; despite the unfortunate turn of events, he wanted to sink himself deep inside Clara as soon as possible.

"Oh, that's good," she said, convincing herself it would all be okay as he reached around her and slid his palms underneath the robe and across her small breasts.

Seven

When they arrived at Eternal Enterprises' hangar, a man in a dark suit was there to greet them. "Who is that?" she whispered to Santino as the man walked toward them. "Detective Flores," Santino answered with a squeeze of her hand.

"Dominic," Santino said when the man approached. They shook hands like friends.

"So, Santino, we need to talk? I hear you are just in from San Francisco?" The detective looked to Clara, waiting to be introduced, but instead Santino gestured toward a leather couch to the side of the hangar.

"I'm sorry, darling, will you give us a moment?"

Clara looked at the detective, then turned to do as Santino asked. She couldn't hear the men talking, but they seemed cordial, friendly even. After a few minutes, a second dark car pulled up and Santino gestured toward it. To her surprise, the detective climbed into the back of the car.

Clara bolted up and walked toward Santino, desperate for news. "Oh my God, the police! Is he here to question you? Don't say anything to him—I know that from Landon, he's almost a cop."

"I didn't picture him as a police officer at all. He seems more like an art major."

"Santino, I'm serious. Don't talk to the cops!"

"Clara, I'm really not sure what has you agitated." He took her hands in his, and raised the right one to his lips. After the kiss, he cradled her hands in his.

"I apologize that I can't take you home personally, my sweet angel, but I have some business with Detective Flores to tend to. Vittoria, my assistant, is in the first car—she will see you safely home."

"Oh, okay, um, I don't need her to take me, I'm fine." Clara couldn't believe that Santino was so calm; as if it were any other Sunday morning, rather than one in which he was about to become a murder suspect.

"I would like to see you again soon—can we have dinner this evening?" Santino's eyes searched hers—he was sad to part with her.

"Um, I have to study tonight, uh, but maybe tomorrow."

"I shall call you, my darling," he said, leaning in to kiss her. "Until then, I shall say good night till it be morrow."

* * * * *

An hour later, after dealing with Detective Flores, Santino sat at the café high atop the Roman across from Nicco. He poured sugar into his tiny cup as he made Nicco wait for the answer to his question. "Ah yes, San Francisco. It was lovely," he eventually answered.

Nicco stared at him, waiting for more. "And the maid?"

Santino nodded as he stirred his espresso. "She is lovely too."

"So before the whole Bay Bridge murder thing ruined your romantic weekend, did she mention the body at the Roman?" Nicco couldn't understand why Santino was being so casual—they were in trouble.

"She did not," Santino said, placing his spoon at the side of his saucer.

"So, do you think we're still okay? She won't talk, right? Even now? Santino, this all too important to risk—"

"I know, Nicco. I certainly didn't plan, or ever expect, this complication with Clara Denton. But now..." He sighed again and shook his head.

"Now you have feelings for her?" Nicco tried to hide his surprise—his best friend, his boss, his prince Santino didn't even *like* humans, even when he was one.

Santino looked at Nicco—he didn't want to have this conversation. "Yes. She's being watched around the clock, correct?"

"She is. That crazy blog guy has been buzzing around her, though."

"That damn Hunter is getting on my nerves. He's far smarter than his father, and that makes him dangerous. He is getting too close to what is mine."

"He's lucky he's dealing with us—there are other families that would be quite dangerous for him." Nicco glanced at his phone—the screen was full of texts, most from Vittoria.

"Indeed," Santino answered. "Speaking of dangerous, the New Orleans witches were in San Francisco. That old hag Fiona confronted me with Clara there. She's lucky she wasn't lying next to that corpse under the bridge."

"What are they doing on this side of the country?" Nicco glanced at his phone again—the latest text from Vittoria was a line of orange angry face emojis. Santino was ignoring her, and she didn't take well to being ignored so she turned to Nicco.

"I don't know, I honestly don't care—but Estrella and her merry band of paranormals had better steer clear of me *and* my girl."

"Your girl," Nicco exclaimed. "Well, this is certainly a new side of you. No wonder Vittoria is so pissed off."

"That ship has long since sailed, my friend."

"I know you don't want to hear this, Santino, but it may be time to move on again. Have we worn out our welcome in Sin City?"

Santino shook his head and pushed back from the table. "Not yet, Nicco, not yet."

* * * * *

"Landon, what should I do?" Clara had been pacing across their tiny living room for the past twenty minutes. On the ride home from the airport, his assistant Vittoria was silent, tapping at her phone and only occasionally looking up to glare at Clara. It was clear the stunning brunette wasn't happy with her boss taking a date to San Francisco for the night. The chill was fine with Clara—she was too busy freaking out to care.

"You should do nothing," Landon answered for the tenth time.

"There was a BLK murder in San Francisco this morning! I saw what I thought was a dead body a week ago in a hotel room, in *Santino's* hotel room, that appeared bloodless. I have to do something." A cold chill ran across her spine. The coincidence startled her, but she also knew what she felt for this man—she was sure he didn't do this.

"A Vegas victim, too," Landon added.

"Yes. He didn't do it; I know he didn't. But this looks *bad.*"

"Clara, you need to stay out of it. Avoid this guy for a while; let things shake out. But *do not* get involved, baby girl." Landon pointed an index finger at her—he knew how her mind worked. Nothing thrilled his best friend more than a true crime story.

"I know, I know. You're right. I'll lie low for a little bit with him," she said, as if she didn't know she wouldn't be able to stay away from Santino. He was all she thought about, and she already yearned for him after only an hour apart.

"Oh, I forgot to tell you. That hunk-a-licious blog guy you met at the restaurant was here last night looking for you. Sure he's not a drop-dead, rich sugar daddy like your serial killing boss, but he's cute. I tried to flirt but got a giant *nada* from him."

"Yeah, his name is Matthew Hunter." Clara glanced at her phone, remembering again that she was supposed to meet him for lunch over the weekend.

"You just have 'em crawling out of the woodwork these days, don't you Clara Belle?"

She tapped at her contacts list to text Matthew, but he wasn't listed. "That's odd, I can't find him," she mumbled, scrolling through her stored numbers.

"Look through your recent calls?" Landon suggested.

"No, there's nothing. It was a Reno number, but I don't see anything other than 702 area codes."

"I bet ol' money bags got jealous and deleted blog boy," Landon said with a wink.

Later, after Landon left for work, she sat at her laptop and searched *Matthew Hunter blogger Reno*. Within seconds, she was at his website. The latest blog post was titled: *Blood Drinkers Rampant in Sin City!* She didn't bother to read it, instead clicking on the link labeled *Stalker Links*.

Within seconds, she'd found Matthew on Facebook and sent him a friend request, only to get an automated message that he'd met his friend limit and she was now following him. "Who has five thousand friends?" she said, clicking on his email link instead.

Hey, it's me, Clara Denton. I'm sorry I flaked on you—something came up. Weirdly I've lost your number, but give me a call sometime and maybe we can try it all again.

Within seconds, he answered.

Clara! Cool. I thought I'd pushed too hard or something. I can't seem to contact you—I thought maybe you'd blocked me. Here's my number...

She called Matthew and they talked for nearly an hour. He could actually be really sweet, and he was funny in his own quirky way. They agreed to meet the next evening to talk, but at the end of the call Matthew said, "Goodbye until our date tomorrow. I'll be praying you don't stand me up again."

Clara had no intention of standing him up, however. When she first spoke to Matthew Hunter, she thought he was nuts. Cute, but nuts. Now, things had gone completely off-kilter and she sensed maybe he wasn't so insane after all. The paranormal she'd never believe in, but something was off and she intended to get answers.

Santino didn't contact her until the next morning. She was just finishing her coffee as her phone rang. Nervously, she answered.

"Hello darling. I've missed you."

"I've missed you, too. I had fun in San Francisco," she said, twisting a lock of her hair nervously.

"I didn't want to bother you last night—you said you had to study. Can we meet tonight, however? I'm dying to see you."

Clara thought for a moment as Santino silently waited for her answer.

"Um, I can't tonight, but maybe tomorrow for lunch?" She was desperate to be near him again, but she wanted to talk to him in a public place. "Can we go someplace other than the Roman?" She wanted to talk to him on neutral turf.

"Of course, my angel. Would you like to try the new French place over at Caesars? I believe they are open for lunch."

Caesars Palace was always bustling with people—she'd be safe there, she thought. "Perfect. Noon?"

"Noon it is, my darling. I shall be counting the seconds."

Clara barely slept that night. She had dreams of Santino—terrifying ones, erotic ones, and her favorite, romantic ones.

As she got ready for lunch the next day, Landon teased her. "Putting on shiny lips for Mr. Rico Suave, are we? Does he know you're also hooking up with the blond in khakis later tonight?"

"Um, no," she confessed. "We're not like exclusive or anything, but I don't think he'd like it."

"Gotcha," Landon said with a wink.

"It's just—we got really close in a short time, or I thought anyway. That day in San Francisco was magical—I know it's corny but it felt like we were soul mates or something. Then everything happened, and I'm just confused."

When Clara walked down the steps leading from her apartment to the parking lot, she saw a dark car at the curb—one of Santino's cars. As she reached the bottom stair, the uniformed driver stepped out and opened the rear door for her.

"Miss," he said as she walked up.

"I-I didn't need a ride." Clara wasn't sure what to do.

"Mr. Marchetti insists."

Clara hesitated, but remembered her gas light had been on for a few days, so she decided to take the free ride to Caesars Palace.

Except, the driver didn't take her to Caesars. Instead, the dark car pulled into a back loading area at the Roman. As the door was opened, Santino stood there smiling, a bouquet of red roses in his left hand.

Clara couldn't help but fall into his arms. He looked beautiful; his crimson tie matched the roses, and when he kissed her, her knees buckled.

"I thought we were meeting there," she said as he took her arm and led her to the private elevator that went to his penthouse.

"I took the liberty of having Rue Marmont send lunch over—more private that way," he said, pulling her closer to him as they rode up.

Clara told herself she wouldn't have sex with him, not until she had some answers, but within minutes of his door closing, she was pulling at his belt. Like a wild animal, she clawed at his clothing, desperate to be as close to him as possible.

"Fuck, Clara, I've missed you," he said, his hands wrapping around her hair as she took him into her mouth.

The food on the counter grew cold as she sucked him, and after he'd pulled back from deep in her throat to come on the tip of her tongue, he pulled her up next to him. As he held her close, his lips grazed her throat. "My sweet angel, I was afraid you were angry with me."

"No, not angry," she said. "Confused, I guess."

"Let me try to clarify things for you, then," he said, lifting her into his arms and carrying her to his bed.

An hour later, he could still taste her sweetness on his tongue as she rolled over to rest her cheek on his chest. "Are we more than just sex, Santino? I know it's only been a very short while, but I need to know. I'm falling hard for you."

His fingertips ran down her back. "I care for you, Clara. I'm not good with talking about feelings, or having them, for that matter. But you have become very special to me in these few days. Yes, we are far more than physical, my darling. And, I will admit, that is new for me."

"For me, too," she confessed, her palm running across his toned chest.

"Be patient with me, angel, I am positive I will make mistakes."

"I was afraid that detective was there to arrest you yesterday," she said, looking up at him to gauge his reaction.

"Arrest me? Why ever would he do that?"

"Well, I mean, we were in another city and there was a murder *there* that matched the serial killings we are having *here*, I was just worried that they might talk to you. Especially after the body at the Roman."

"There was no body at the Roman." Clara felt his body tense; she sensed that he was lying, or at least hiding something.

"Santino, listen, if it comes to it, I'll tell them that I was with you the whole time, you know, in San Francisco."

He jolted up, causing her to roll off of him. "Why the hell would you do that? Lie for me, is that what you're saying?"

She sat up and pulled the sheet around her. "Um, yeah, I mean I was just saying that if you needed—"

"An alibi?" he hissed.

"Yeah, that." She had no idea what she'd done wrong.

"Clara, I don't need a fake alibi. But the fact that you do means you think *I* killed those women!"

"No, I just, I'm sorry."

"As am I," was all he said before getting into the shower.

Eight

"**Y**our boyfriend is a killer."
Matthew's eyes met hers from across the table later that night.

"He's not my boyfriend," was the only thing she could say in protest.

He shoved a limp fry into his mouth. With a grimace, he quipped, "You don't bother denying that he's a murderer then?"

Clara sighed and sank back into the plastic chair. With a long sip of her milkshake, she studied him. Matthew Hunter was cute, and smart, a little crazy, but exactly her type of guy. But she knew there was a force that would keep her from ever being with this quirky blond. That force, she knew, was Santino. She glanced at her phone for the hundredth time—there was nothing from him.

"Look at this," Matthew said suddenly. Clara reached for the piece of printer paper he slid across the table toward her.

The image, a printout of a painting that hung in the Louvre in Paris, bore his exact likeness. Her heart thumped in her chest as she willed herself to be calm, to think. "An ancestor," she finally said out loud. "He said he came from a very old family back in Italy."

"Did he say Italy?" Matthew's lips curled into a smug grin.

"Well, no, I think he said Rome."

"Right. Well, when he was there, *Italy* didn't exist."

"That's not possible. Listen, Matthew, just the other day I saw some hundred-year-old picture that looked just like Jimmy Fallon. This might be his family, even though it says Medici, or it's a freaky coincidence." She looked again at the painting and wondered if Matthew was trying to trick her. It looked *just* like Santino.

"Clara, have you ever tried to Google him? There are no pictures of Santino Marchetti, owner of several resort properties around the world. You don't find that odd?"

"Well, I mean, he's reclusive for sure."

"Clara, wake up. He can't be photographed! He's a vampire."

Clara slid the paper back toward Matthew and began to gather her garbage. "I like you Matthew, I do, but this has gone far enough." Before he could speak, she'd left the table. He watched her leave, unsure of what to do. He liked her, but he wouldn't stop warning her about the blood-drinker he feared she was sleeping with.

* * * * *

She knew Matthew would follow her, so the second she made it to her car she pulled out of the parking lot and joined the masses of cars clogging Harmon Avenue to leave the Strip that night. At the first stoplight she pulled out her phone and flipped through her pictures until she saw it. She'd stared at the image since that night in San Francisco when she'd taken it.

A honk behind her jolted her, and she dropped her phone in the passenger seat and began to creep forward at the green light. "He's not a vampire, that's crazy," she said out loud to the empty car. "I have a picture of him," she reassured herself as her hand began to shake. He'd never let her take a selfie with him, or any photo. At first she'd worried it was because he was ashamed of being with her, that he didn't want a picture of himself with a common hotel maid on Instagram. But now, after what Matthew had said, she was thoroughly confused.

At the next stoplight, in a hasty burst of anger, she texted the profile picture of Santino in the moonlight to Matthew with the simple message:

You read too many horror books. He CAN be photographed!

* * * * *

She texted Santino that night, but he didn't answer.

The next morning, there was still no answer. Clara started to panic—she'd lost him, lost him before she really even had him. She sent another text as she got ready for work. A simple one, with only the words *I'm sorry.*

Mid-afternoon, Matthew Hunter called. "Please Clara, go out with me. Just for fun, I promise. You're the only girl I know in Vegas."

She'd agreed, mostly because she had so many questions, and even Matthew's half-baked theories were better than the void she felt.

That evening Clara sat across the sticky pub table from Matthew. She still hadn't heard from Santino, and her texts were read but unanswered. With a clench of her gut, she slid the phone back into her pocket. *Either she truly was just a fling to him or she'd hurt him badly with her mistrust,* she thought as Matthew tapped at his phone screen.

He was cute, and nice—and, he seemed to be into her. Clara wanted to like him—she *did* like him, but all she could think about was Santino.

"Hey, I thought we could go live from here— my followers would eat that with a spoon," he said with a wide grin.

She stared at her menu, eventually asking, "What does that mean? *Go live?*" Clara was often bored by Matthew's talk of posts, followers, and something called click bait. She knew very little about social media, and really only used the internet via her iPhone to pay bills, when she had the cash, and to search for news about the latest crime story she was addicted to.

"Uh, you know, broadcast live on Facebook. By the way, I can't find your Instagram account. They'd love it that I'm dating an actual player in the vampire murders."

She'd had enough, and with the sharp slam of her heavy menu to the table, she went off. "I'm not on Instagram, there are no vampires, and we're *not* dating." Her eyes leveled at him, her lips pursed into a sneer. He was sweet, and cute as hell, but she wasn't in the mood for his obsession with the paranormal.

Matthew put his phone away, and reached a hand toward her, pulling it back suddenly at the fear of touching her. The Hunter had scores of virtual friends, even many fangirls who fawned over him, but real, live women terrified him.

"I'm sorry, that didn't come out the way I meant it. Yeah, I mean it started with my interest in the killings and your role in it, but I've really, I mean, I like you. I care, Clara," he said, his palms in the air.

Clara searched his eyes—he was afraid, afraid and nervous. "Please," he said so quietly it was almost a prayer.

Her hand reached across to his, and she felt a rush of warmth at the first touch they'd shared. *If it weren't for Santino then maybe*, she thought.

"Clara, I get nervous around you, say dumb stuff." His fingers wrapped around hers. "I'm sorry I'm such an idiot," he said with a squeeze of her hand.

At least he's honest, she thought. "Okay, let's get out of here, Matthew. This place is over-priced—who cares about some TV chef? There's a new In-N-Out Burger down by the LINQ—I could use a Double Double."

It was a nice night, so they took their greasy sack of burgers and fries to a bench in the center of the pedestrian area that stretched between the LINQ and Flamingo casinos—a popular place for tourists and locals alike to stroll on any given evening. A nearby guitarist belted out pop songs for tips while security kept a close eye on the unauthorized buskers and costumed-entertainers vying for tourist money. At the end of the LINQ promenade sat a recent addition to the Las Vegas skyline—the giant High Roller wheel, larger even than its sister structure, the London Eye. Clara munched her limp fries as she watched the wheel change colors.

"There's no such thing as vampires, Matthew," she said absently, determined to not be sitting next to a total maniac.

He sighed and sipped hard on his chocolate shake. "I understand it's hard to believe," was all he could manage to say. The things he knew she couldn't comprehend; he could accept that.

She reached for her shake, vanilla, and as she raised the straw to her lips, he leaned in, nearly knocking the straw from her hands. "Oh, sorry," he chirped, embarrassed at his failed attempt at a kiss. It had been a year since Matthew had kissed anyone, and even then, that date didn't go beyond that.

With a swipe of the vanilla ice cream from her lips, she leaned in to Matthew. This guy was normal, well except for all of his insanity, and more importantly, he seemed to like her, murder witness or not. Santino was ignoring her, may never speak to her again—so she decided to act.

With a lunge, she pressed her lips to his, the sweetness of the chocolate causing her to push harder.

Matthew's heart pounded as he fought for the courage to open his lips to hers, to deepen the kiss. He felt himself harden uncomfortably as Clara's arm snaked around his back.

As her tongue slid into his mouth, her phone vibrated in her pocket. *Santino!* The name rang through her brain like a chant, and as much as she fought to continue to kiss Matthew, her fingers flew to the phone.

"I'm sorry, my roommate is sick, I wanted to make sure he didn't need me," she lied.

Matthew felt the pang of disappointment as Clara swiped at her phone. "Oh, no worries, just one of those silly texts about my Old Navy rewards expiring," she explained. Now *she* was the disappointed one.

He reached for her hand again. "Gotta love Old Navy," he said with the shake of his head.

"I need to get home—but I really did have a good time tonight. Thanks for dinner," she said as she stood. With a crumple of the greasy white bag, he smiled at her. Her hair shined in the artificial lights of the night—he wanted nothing more than to kiss her again.

"Tomorrow maybe?"

She paused for a moment. "Oh yeah, how about around two? I have to work in the morning, but I get paid tomorrow. We can have lunch—my treat."

Matthew was close to broke, but he was old-fashioned. "No, I can't do that. I get my royalty deposit tomorrow—we'll have a proper meal. Deal?"

She nodded and drew closer to him. "It's a deal." In a burst of confidence she rarely felt, she kissed him one more time before feeling her phone vibrate again.

"Roommate?" he asked, the warmth of the kiss glowing within him.

"Probably just my Kohl's cash expiring," she joked. "I had a good time, Matthew. I'll see you tomorrow."

"Such sweet sorrow," he said as she turned to go.

"I love Shakespeare," she sighed as she left him and walked through the throng of tipsy tourists toward the Roman where her car sat in the employee lot.

The light was dim, but she saw the dark figure leaning against the trunk of her car. Her heart pounded out a rhythm she'd never known. *Santino!*

"Have fun with the psycho, Clara?" His tone was cold as she came within feet of him. She laced her keys through her fingers as she'd learned years prior in a women's defense course in school.

"Why do you care? Were you spying on me?"

"Spying?"

She ignored him and reached for her car door.

"We need to talk." His hand grabbed her wrist and held her still—he was close enough for her to smell his cologne. Time seemed to stop as they stood there—the scratchy wool of his suit coat brushed against her wrist. "I've been trying to talk to you for days, and you've shut me out!" she screamed.

"So you fell into bed with someone else?"

"What's it to you?" she hissed, pulling away from him. "I'll call security," she warned, her voice shaky.

"I own security, my doubting angel." His voice was low, pained. "I just want to make sure you're safe. I would never hurt you, Clara."

She yanked her wrist from his grasp. "You already have," she shot out as she pulled open her car door and flung herself inside.

He watched as she drove off, followed by the security guard who'd been protecting her since the day she saw the body in the hotel room. Santino shook as it ran through his mind again: the image of his Clara kissing the Hunter was more than he could bear.

Hours later, when she'd dried her tears, she pulled out her phone to set an alarm. There was a text from Matthew, telling her how much he enjoyed his time with her and how he couldn't wait until their next meeting.

But what made her blood run white-hot, what made her shake, was the text before that—the one that had come while she kissed Matthew goodbye.

It was from Santino and read:

Sweet, so would I. Yet I should kill thee with much cherishing. Good night, good night! Parting is such sweet sorrow.

Clara knew the line from *Romeo and Juliet* well, but what caused her to fly up in her bed was the realization that the text came through *before* Matthew had said the same words to her.

Nine

"Of course I'll rub bones with him," Vittoria said, pacing in front of Santino's desk.

"I said meet with him. Find out what he knows; what he's doing with my Clara."

"*I* was once yours, my prince. It wasn't all bad."

He refilled his glass of wine from the crystal carafe. "You know I love you," he said as he took a long drink.

She stopped pacing and stood across from him. "And I you, Santino, always. I'm at your service, but it hurts to see you once again involved with a human. Have you forgotten what we did? We promised each other—never again."

He sat on the edge of his desk. "I know. I've already lost her anyway—she doesn't trust me. She thinks I'm a murderer. But, please Vittoria, I can't have her with *him*."

"Tell her the truth then, my prince."

The next day, Clara was called up to his office. She thought about not going up for a split second, but she had to see him. When Vittoria led her from the reception area to his office, Santino was standing at the wall of windows, staring out at the bustling tourism below. Human activity always calmed him.

"I was hurt that you would think that of me," he said as he heard the door close.

"I know," she began, fighting the tears that threatened to fall. "It was stupid."

He turned to her and slipped his hands into his pockets. He'd never been so happy to see a human, or anyone that he could remember, in his entire life. Without her, he couldn't breathe.

"Clara, I understand though. The coincidence, all of it, to you it must look, well, I can certainly concede that things became bizarre. I didn't kill those women."

"I know," she said through her tears. She moved closer to him—she yearned to be in his arms again. "I read too many true crime books, I got paranoid that they would pin this on you, I just panicked. I am so sorry; please forgive me, Santino."

"Clara, I haven't told you this. I believe someone is trying to make it appear that I *am* the Blood Lust Killer. San Francisco was not a coincidence."

Before she could process what Santino was saying, a door opened from the side of the room and Nicco walked in.

"I apologize, Miss Denton, it's urgent that I have a quick word with Santino," he said.

"Give me a few seconds, Nicco."

Nicco nodded and smiled at Clara before turning to leave. His face glowed, his brown hair shone in the lights of the office—Nicco reminded her of Superman. His build was powerful, but his expression was one of eternal joy.

Nicco left through the same door he'd entered from. Santino turned to Clara.

"For him to interrupt, it must be important. I am sorry, my darling, but we do need to talk. Can we meet this evening?"

"Am I forgiven, then? I mean, are we, are we okay?"

He took her into his arms and gave her a quick squeeze before guiding her toward the door. "I need you, Clara Denton, but we need to talk. I'd hoped it could wait until further into our, our relationship I guess is the right word, but events have not cooperated. Tonight, I will tell you everything, and I fear more than anything that after I bare my soul you will never want to see me again."

* * * * *

Vittoria didn't see the messages on her phone from her friend Jenna, the receptionist who possessively controlled access to the executive offices at the Roman. She was too busy staring into his eyes that afternoon. The young man was talking, but she wasn't listening. She was too busy imagining him in bed on top of her, those eyes the color of the ultramarine blue in a Rubens painting looking into hers as he drove her to ecstasy.

"So you see," the Hunter said, "your boss is one of them. He's a blood drinker, and you are in grave danger."

"Interesting," Vittoria purred as her foot found the hem of his khaki trousers.

"You think I'm nuts," he said before taking a giant swig of his beer.

"I think you're cute," she said as her foot slid up the leg of his pants.

"Uh, seriously, though. This isn't a game," he scolded.

Matthew shifted in his chair as her bare toe caressed his calf. As the waitress approached, he tossed a napkin over his lap to hide his erection.

"Well, Mr. Hunter, I am Marchetti's personal assistant, so I have access to *everything*. Perhaps, after a few more drinks, I can have one of the drivers pick us up and we can snoop around his chambers?"

Sweat beads dotted across Matthew's forehead. "Well, I mean, if you think we could?"

She ran her toe up to his knee. "I heard a rumor that he wears some black cape, and also that there are bats occasionally around his bedroom."

Matthew wiped his forehead with the napkin. "You're teasing me," he said.

"I have not yet *begun* to tease you, sexy boy," Vittoria answered with a lick of her lips.

* * * * *

"Holy crud, this is really it?" Matthew looked around at the elegant apartment, located near the top of the Roman.

"So, what is it you wanted to see, exactly?" Vittoria asked as she made her signature drink at the marble wet bar.

"Oh, I don't even know, really. I mean I should know, but—wow, this is just incredible. Are you sure we're safe?" Matthew felt a tremor run down his spine—he was excited; excited and terrified.

"Quite safe. They call me when Mr. Marchetti leaves his office so I can prepare. It's usually quite late in the night." Vittoria poured another glug of alcohol into her glass.

"Prepare?"

"Of course. I have to choose which virgin he will drain of blood each evening." Her bright red lips curled at the edges as she waited for Matthew's reaction.

"You're teasing me again," he said with a wink.

"Drink? Tito's and tonic, you'll love it."

"Uh, no, vodka gives me heartburn," he said flatly. He walked toward the bedroom and stood in the doorway with his back to Vittoria.

She set the drink down and walked toward him, wrapping her arms around his waist. "Enough teasing—let's fuck."

"Uh, I-I um..."

She moved her hand lower until it grasped the hard bulge in his signature khaki pants. "You don't want to?" Her lips moved to his neck, the thump of his blood making her ache with desire.

"I do, I'm just not sure why someone like you would want someone like me." He turned around to face her. Women like Vittoria intimidated him. Once, in high school, he'd been the target of the age-old prank of the hot girl asking out the nerd on a dare. Whenever an attractive, confident woman like Vittoria showed interest, he assumed it was a joke.

"I will have you, Matthew Hunter. The first time those warm blue eyes met mine, I knew we'd be together. But we don't need to rush—I just want to get to know you better."

He relaxed a little. "I'd like that. Can we start by ending the lies though?"

She took a deep breath and walked back to her couch. Vittoria kicked off her stilettos and patted the seat next to her.

When he joined her, she laid her head in his lap. As his fingers wound through her hair, she began. "This is my place. Santino lives upstairs in the penthouse."

"I'd gathered that much," he answered. "Do you think I'm crazy? I mean Clara doesn't believe a word of what I know."

"Clara," she repeated. "Are you two...involved? You know he's obsessed with her, right?"

"I know, yeah. We kissed once, went out a few times, but nothing ever clicked. I do worry about her, though. And I worry about you. He's a monster, Vittoria."

"I like you, Matthew, but please don't use that word about him. Santino is more than my boss—he's my best friend, so this could get complicated."

"You haven't once denied it."

"Matthew, *please.*" She rose up to look into his eyes.

His fingertips brushed across her cheek. "I *can* promise that tonight will only be about us."

The nerves faded away as his lips met hers. He no longer cared why she wanted him, just that she did.

An hour later, as she untied the Hunter's wrists from her headboard, his curious eyes studied her. "That was certainly, well, I've never done *that.*"

Vittoria looked over at him—naked, sweaty, and perfect. "I'm glad you liked it—I can whip you if you'd like? Just for fun, of course."

"Um, no," he said with a nervous chuckle as he rubbed the circulation back into his wrists. "Do you always go to such extremes to avoid connecting during sex?"

Her eyes shot to his, then darted away the second their gaze met. What started as obedience to Santino, and the desire for a quick romp with the cute blond, had taken a turn she never expected.

"Listen, Matthew, I'm not really looking for anything more than a good time—that's all I can handle right now." She needed to get away from his eyes, from that knowing look that tore through her like a bullet.

"There's something about you, Vittoria. You hide behind this cold, sexy façade, but underneath it all, we aren't that different, are we?"

"How are we possibly alike?"

"We're both hunting something we haven't been able to find—our whole lives."

"I'm not chasing Santino Marchetti, if that's what you mean." She sat on the bed next to him, unable to fight the urge to touch him for one more second.

"Maybe not, but how long has it been since someone saw past the mask and really got to know you?"

She looked at the ceiling—she had to get away from him. The Hunter was peering into her soul. "Oh, I don't know, decades I suppose."

He grinned as he pulled her close to him. "Can we just slow down a little and see what the afternoon holds? No more talk of vampires and blood sucking bosses—just you and me, as human beings hanging out?"

"Human beings," she repeated as her lips found his neck.

"All of the kink was mind-blowing, Vittoria, it really was—but for round two, can I show you what I can do?"

She nodded as his fingertips raised her chin to his. That afternoon, when Matthew Hunter kissed her again, she felt her entire universe shift—and it both thrilled and terrified her as she thought back to the past—to the broken heart that never really healed after all these years.

* * * * *

That evening, Vittoria sat next to Matthew Hunter at a popular chain restaurant, her hand on his knee. The theme seemed to be some brewery, and she squinted as she surveyed the long list of beers on tap. "Get that Brunette one," Matthew said pointing at the chalkboard on the wall. "It reminds me of you." He squeezed her hand—despite the shock of a body in San Francisco, he was bubbling over with excitement. This beautiful creature was into him, really into him. Surely his luck with women was about to change.

"What is it you do for a living, Victoria?" his Aunt Janet asked from across the table. When his aunt and uncle heard he was seeing someone, they insisted on taking the two of them out, their treat, to get to know her better.

"*Vittoria,* actually, ma'am. It's an old Roman name. I'm the personal assistant to the owner of the Roman hotel and casino," she answered.

Matthew's aunt nodded to her husband, John. Vittoria's old-fashioned manners impressed them.

The waitress interrupted, and when Vittoria ordered her steak "as rare as she could get it," the woman seemed flustered. "Oh, okay, of course," she mumbled as she scurried away.

"So this man you work for, he's quite reclusive I hear?" John asked.

Matthew nearly spilled his beer at the mention of Santino.

Vittoria, however, was perfectly comfortable discussing him. "He's very private, yes. I got the job because our parents are both from the same neighborhood in Rome."

"It's a beautiful place, the Roman. We had our book group's Christmas party there last year—just phenomenal."

"Aunt Janet," Matthew interrupted, "I told you about that place! Vittoria won't listen either, but mark my words, that place is evil."

"Oh baby, don't be silly," Vittoria said, her hand creeping up his thigh to rest along his zipper. "Santino Marchetti is a good man, and there is no evil at the Roman."

"Blood drinkers right under your nose, and none of you will see it," Matthew grumbled under his breath as his uncle ordered another round of drinks.

Vittoria smiled at Matthew. She adored this silly human in a way she hadn't in forever—but she would not let her mind even think about Howard. The memory of him was far too painful—and besides, she would never let it get that serious with Matthew Hunter.

*****

At a quarter to ten the next morning, Clara raced toward the changing room to get into uniform. At the Roman, housekeeping wore designer uniforms from Italy, but they weren't allowed to leave the premises. From the rack, she pulled a ladies size four and slipped into it as quickly as she could. As always, she was late. As she grabbed her cleaning basket to service her assigned rooms, however, her supervisor stood in front of her like a brick wall.

"Miss Lopez, uh, is something wrong?"

"*Is something wrong,*" the woman mocked like a kindergartener on the playground.

"I-I promise I'll work on getting here earlier, ma'am. It's just I have European History before this, and the professor always goes long." Clara tried to maneuver around the woman, but Miss Lopez took a step to block her.

"College girl, I see. So to you, privileged white college girl, this is just a stepping stone, beer money? This is as much as I will ever get—I graduated college, though, for your information. In Guadalajara—so yes, that gets me as far in America as watching over lazy maids clean the rooms of the rich."

"I'm sorry," was all Clara could think to say.

But what she wouldn't say raced through her mind. *White, yes, and college? I'll leave the University of Nevada Las Vegas, ma'am, with about seventy thousand dollars of student debt. I'll make about twenty-five thousand a year working some county job teaching or at some library if I go for a Masters degree, if I'm lucky enough to get a job at all. And yes, my skin is white, but my parents were both junkies and there were many days where I ate by pilfering others' school lunches or digging through the Burger King dumpster behind our apartment. Privileged my ass.*

"Well, Clara, you don't have to be sorry, or be on time for that matter. To be honest, I'm not really sure why you even bother showing up. When you're fucking the boss, life is good apparently."

* * * * *

138

It happened in the middle of her second room. One of the laundry guys, Juan, dropped off the fresh sheets just as she clicked on the TV. "Oh, look, he struck again!" Juan shouted, pointing at the screen.

Clara turned to look, her hands busy unfolding the linens. She froze when she saw the face on the local news. A reporter was speaking, and she turned up the volume, struggling to understand what was happening.

> *"That's right, Brian, we are hearing today from Metro that the body found in the alley behind the strip club is indeed that of missing New Yorker Joan Allen. It appears to be drained of its blood, however at this time Metro is not confirming that this is yet another victim of the Blood Lust Killer."*

"They better catch that boy," Juan said as he gathered up the dirty sheets to take back to the laundry facility.

Clara stood frozen as they showed the snapshot of the victim, Joan Allen. She'd never forget that face, although it looked much different alive than it did pale and dead that night at the Roman. Santino lied to her—the body she saw that night was very much real, and very much dead.

Her legs gave way as the image of the victim faded to a press conference with a suited detective answering questions. It was the same man she'd seen at

Santino's hangar at the airport the day they returned from San Francisco, Detective Flores.

"The victim has been dead for some time, we believe, but the coroner will conduct a thorough examination. Yes, this does appear to be in line with the style of the BLK killings the city has been plagued with, but it's too early to tell."

She left the room half cleaned and headed as quickly as she could to get her things and change out of the maid uniform, praying her supervisor wasn't around. She expected to see Santino as she reached her car, but the garage was empty. Her iPhone had no messages. The entire world just fell apart, and she seemed to be the only one to care.

It was late evening before he called.

"My angel, I'd hoped to talk to you before that unfortunate story made the news." He was silent, waiting.

"Unfortunate story?" she hissed.

"Darling, let me explain, please. I've sent a car for you; it's out front. I shall tell you everything."

"Go fuck yourself."

"Clara, that was rude. I deserve more respect than that. Get in the car."

"Sorry, go fuck yourself, Mister Serial Killer."

She ended the call, expecting him to pursue her, but he didn't.

After half an hour, the black car rolled away. In a fit, desperate for something from him, she texted him:

I saw the blood stained shirt! Is that what she was wearing? Joan? The night you murdered her at the Roman?

He never answered.

Hours later, Landon came home from work with a foil container of lasagna. "Look baby girl, I even got salad," he said as he peeled the foil lid back. "We'll eat veggies tonight, can you believe it?"

"We'll starve once you're a cop," she said, her mind on Santino.

As Landon searched for wine, Clara picked at the lasagna with her fork. Even though her stomach howled, the only thought she had about the food was the amount of garlic, and that Santino would offer her a stick of cinnamon, always cinnamon, gum if he smelled it on her breath.

As a tear rolled down her cheek, she thought about the possibility that she'd never see him again.

"What's wrong, Clara Belle?" Landon asked as he turned around with their wine in red Solo cups.

"I accused him of being a murderer."

"Well that can be a sure trust issue in a relationship. Is this about the body found today?"

Landon sat across from her at their battered table.

"Yes, that woman, it's the same...I mean that is the corpse I saw at the Roman!" She took a deep breath, feeling relieved that it was out. She had to tell someone.

"That's messed up," was all he said.

"And the other day in his guest room I found a stained shirt—stained *bright red.*"

"Did you ask Sir Dark and Dominant about it?"

"Well, no, but I just—it freaked me out a little. There's also his writings."

"Writings?" Landon shoved a heaping fork full of lasagna into his mouth.

"He has this journal type thing. Like the other day, one of them was about washing blood from his hands, and before there was one that said 'Blood will have blood.' How creepy is that?"

"Clara," Landon said with a sigh, "you read too much true crime. You of all people should recognize that line—I'm pretty sure it's Shakespeare."

"*Macbeth,*" she said, suddenly placing the line, remembering that golden afternoon in San Francisco when they'd admired the copies of the play at the rare books store on Geary Street.

"What about the blood stained shirt?"

Landon leaned back in his chair and tossed a soggy crouton into his mouth. "I may just be a cadet, but it seems to me that if he were drinking the victim's blood, as the coroner suspects the killer is doing, there wouldn't be blood soaked clothing lying around. You didn't mention seeing blood anywhere that day at the Roman. And if he hid the body of the chick at the Roman, why take her shirt and put it in a guest room in his house? It doesn't make sense."

It didn't make sense. Even worse, inside she knew he wasn't the killer. But she knew he was lying to her, about the body, clearly, but also about more. There was a part of him that he kept from her.

"I'm going to talk to Matthew I think." She looked again at her phone—no messages.

"He's a bit loony. I think you should talk to Santino the Sexy himself. Meet him in public if you're afraid, but I do think you should talk it out a little before you call Metro and have him locked up."

"I'd never do that!"

Landon raised his eyebrow. "You would if you thought he was the Blood Lust Killer."

She slammed down her fork. "I know! I don't think that. I'm just confused. Why did he have the body moved?"

"Ask him. The other thing, my little Sherlock Holmes, was the blood stain on the shirt dry or wet?"

"Uh, dry."

Landon nodded. "And you said earlier it was bright red? The stain?"

She nodded.

"Dried blood on a white shirt would look brownish, not bright red. Isn't ol' boy a big wine loving type? Sounds like he might have had too much vino or something," Landon said with a long sip of his own plastic cup of wine.

"Nothing makes sense," Clara said, fighting the urge to call him.

* * * * *

The next day, she noticed she was being followed. Everywhere she went, a man in a dark shirt and jeans, freshly pressed jeans, was there. The man tried to blend in, but he stood out like a sore thumb on campus.

Worried, she called Matthew. They met at the Starbucks on the corner that afternoon. The pressed jeans guy was there minutes later, trying to look casual as he surveyed the travel mugs for sale.

"Yeah, that guy—I mean holy crap, the police are following me!" She pried the lid off of her latte to let it cool.

"Him? Clara, that's no cop. That dude is wearing a five hundred dollar pair of shoes. He's either CIA or private security, I'd guess. You're sure he's following you?"

She nodded.

"Listen, I hate to bring this up, but are you sure it's not your undead boyfriend having you followed? That looks like a guy in his price range for sure." Matthew slathered butter on his slab of banana walnut bread as he watched the man, who was now reading the back of a box of K-Cups.

"Santino won't talk to me. I-I called him a murderer."

Matthew snorted and shook his head. "Finally she sees the light," he said with a whistle. "Listen, I have books I've written on these blood drinkers, information you'll need. What's your Kindle address? I'll send copies direct to there."

She stared at him. "I have no idea what you mean. I don't have a Kindle."

"But you read, I mean, you read like crazy. What do you read on?"

"I read books, mostly borrowed from the library. Once in a while I have the budget to buy something."

He shook his head again and said under his breath, "Hard copies, wow. Okay, then, my old-fashioned friend, I'll print out some information for you."

"Wait, what are we talking about? Not vampires again."

"Yes, Santino is one of them. But, Clara, I must admit—I do know that he's not the serial killer."

"I know that, I mean in my heart I just know it. But I got confused, scared, and said horrible things to him." She took a long sip of her still-too-hot latte.

"Well, he is a monster, so don't feel bad. At least you're away from him before it's too late. I keep trying to convince Vittoria of that but she won't listen."

"You spoke to her? His assistant?"

Matthew leaned in and whispered, "We're kind of an item."

Clara fought the urge to chuckle—she was sure the sexy siren Vittoria had nothing for her geeky friend. "You said you know he's not the serial killer. How?"

Matthew wiped the stickiness of the banana bread from his fingers, pausing as he decided how much he wanted to reveal to Clara. The sadness in her eyes was more than he could bear, so despite his reservations, he told her what he knew.

"You proved to me that I was wrong about photographs. Vampires can appear on digital images, at least."

"Oh my God, Santino isn't a—"

"Never mind that for now," Matthew interrupted. "Anyway, that got me thinking. I have a buddy that works for the CHP over in Oakland. He saw the CCTV footage of the murderer placing the body of that murder victim under the bridge."

"Holy crap," Clara said.

"It was fuzzy, and the guy wore a big coat and some sort of ski mask over his head and face, but he was s*hort*, Clara."

"Santino's not that tall, I mean he's about your height, maybe six foot two?"

"For his kind, Santino is crazy tall. This guy was probably five-five or so at best. Clara, it wasn't him."

"You're sure?" She felt her heart lift; she needed confirmation of what she already knew.

He nodded. "There's more." Matthew leaned in and lowered his voice to a whisper. "I know a kid who hacks into the police networks. The guy at the coffee shop has store camera footage that clearly shows Santino there during the time the body was placed."

Clara felt a wave of relief rush over her. "I knew he had no part in it!"

"Wait, I didn't say that. I think he's clearly covering it up—he knows it was one of his coven, maybe even who. Why else would he move the body from the Roman?"

She leaned back in her chair again. "Well, if that's true then why did the body reappear? Why didn't he get rid of it?"

Matthew searched for an answer, but didn't have one. "I don't know."

* * * * *

She hadn't been to work in a week, and yet they didn't call. To her surprise, her paycheck was deposited into her nearly empty bank account as if she'd been clocking in. Clara went to class, and to see her mother a few times, but other than that all of her spare time was spent crying; crying and staring at her one picture of Santino. She'd felt something with him that she'd never felt before, and yet, she knew he wasn't telling her the truth.

When the text came through, she jumped. Aside from one call after she'd stormed out, he'd made no attempt to contact her. She glanced at it, reading it several times before the words took meaning.

> *Clara, please meet me. We need to talk. I can explain. – S.*

He was so formal, she thought. *Who signs a text?*

She ignored it; at least for ten whole minutes while she walked in circles around her apartment. Then, she tapped out a response.

I have nothing to say left.

Crap! Why do I not read it before I press send? She saw he was typing but hurriedly made the correction.

I mean I have nothing left to stay.

"Damn! Another typo, I did it again," she screamed at the walls. As her fingers raced to type again, he answered.

My darling, there's an eternity left to say.

Clara reached for the fridge and pulled out the five-dollar bottle of wine Landon bought earlier at CVS. She poured the pink liquid into a jam jar glass she'd had since the ninth grade and took a long drink of the sweet fluid. *Never,* her mind said, but her heart knew she wanted to see Santino again.

Meet me.

She nearly spilled her wine as the new text buzzed her iPhone. This time, she answered honestly, the warmth of the wine making her brave.

I want to, but I'm afraid.

His response was quick.

Me too. Where and when?

She finished the glass, and before she could stop herself, tapped out the reply.

At the Flamingo Garden, tomorrow morning at ten.

She refilled her glass as she waited for him to answer. But he didn't.

* * * * *

Clara sat on the stone bench near the Flamingo Garden at the iconic Flamingo casino in the heart of the Strip. She went there often—mostly because it was free. Her stepfather had once been a Blackjack dealer there, before he was fired, and her mother slung cocktails in a skimpy outfit for tip money years ago. She both loved and hated the Flamingo, and the same could be said of how she felt about her parents.

He was there, even though she'd arrived a full thirty minutes early. She felt him, even though she couldn't see him. He was there, watching her, from somewhere. At exactly ten that morning, Santino sat down on the bench next to her. Her heart thumped against her ribcage as she forced herself to look at him. Santino wore his usual dark suit, made in Rome just for him. The maroon tie laid flatly against his starched white shirt—also custom made, as were his shoes, although he had all of his leather designed in Florence. He took a deep breath and turned toward her.

His jet-black hair brushed against his right eyebrow. Clara noticed that Santino's hair always seemed as if it were just in need of a cut, but never seemed to be any longer or any shorter than it was at that very moment. The scruffy beard was always of exactly the same density—never fuller, never less. The sound of his voice lulled her as he began to speak. "Clara, please let me explain. I care for you deeply, I don't want to lose you."

"You already have," she said, the tears catching in her throat. "You lied to me from the beginning, and you covered up a murder."

"I didn't cover it up, I just used some contacts I have with Metro to move it to another location. I couldn't keep her death secret forever, though. Her family deserved closure. I'd hoped to find the courage to tell you before you heard it elsewhere, however."

His hand reached for hers, and although she knew she should, she didn't resist. They sat in silence for several long moments as various tourists stared at them, perplexed by the handsome, rich businessman holding hands with a young woman in tattered jeans, laceless sneakers, and an Imagine Dragons concert t-shirt.

When the tourists moved on from the curiosity of the scene, Santino spoke again, his voice so low she had to strain to hear him.

"I didn't murder those women. How could you think that I did? This is what this is about, right? You didn't leave me over a lie, you left because you thought I was a killer."

"I know you are not *the* serial killer, Santino. But you *are* a killer, aren't you?"

"How can you say that?"

"Stop lying to me. Have you ever killed anyone?" She pulled her hand from his and turned to face him.

There was a darkness to his eyes as he said, "Yes."

"When? Why?"

His lungs filled with air as he studied her. Santino was on the edge of an abyss, and one more step would throw them both into it forever; the consequences of his decision were enormous. And yet, he knew he couldn't lose her.

"I'll tell you, everything—the truth. But not here, not in public." He glanced around the garden, his eyes once again catching the sight of the man he knew as the Hunter hiding behind a giant palm. He could only hope Vittoria had him under control.

"You just told me you've killed another human, and now you're asking me to go off with you—alone?"

He took her hand once again. "Yes."

* * * * *

It was easy to lose Matthew. Santino had a car waiting at the VIP entrance to the casino, whereas Matthew's battered truck was in the sprawling self-parking garage. By the time Matthew made it out of the Flamingo and onto Las Vegas Boulevard, they were already in Santino's penthouse—alone.

"Wine?" Santino asked, already pouring two glasses of the best cabernet he had upstairs. Clara sat on the sofa staring out at the city down below. She wasn't afraid—but she sensed her life was about to change forever. There was no going back from Santino.

He handed her the glass and sat on the ottoman across from her. "I don't know where to begin," he said after a gulp of the wine.

"From the beginning?"

He turned even paler than normal. "I'm not ready for that. Can we start with Las Vegas?"

She nodded. "Okay, how long have you been in Vegas?"

"Since 1952," he answered.

"And you were how old?" Clara struggled to stay calm, to resist the urge to run.

"Thirty-two. The same as now, Clara. I've always been thirty-two."

She set the wine on the glass coffee table and walked to the wall of windows.

"So you were thirty-two when you, when you, um, died?"

"Yes." He was at her shoulder—she hadn't heard him get up or walk toward her. Santino moved more silently than anyone she'd ever known. *Than anyone ever could,* she thought.

"Let's get some air." He led her to the terrace. "Our first kiss was at this very railing," he said.

"I'll never forget.

"You mentioned the dating TV show, with the roses."

"Santino, I-I'm so confused." He felt her doubt, her disbelief, and couldn't blame her.

He nodded and stepped up onto the narrow railing in a motion so fast, she barely saw him scale it. Balancing on the six-inch ledge, he looked over at Clara. "I could just be insane, or trying to trick you for some sick reason, or maybe it's true, and everything you believed, everything you thought you knew, just turned upside down."

"Please come down," she said as he walked along the narrow ledge. "I-I know there's something, I mean, yeah you're different. But it's just all so crazy; I just can't believe it.

"I didn't believe any of it either." He leaned over the edge—sixty-seven floors down, humans were everywhere, like bees from a disturbed hive.

"Come off the edge, I believe you," she begged. Her hand fished around her pocket for her phone—should she call the police?

"If you believed me, my angel, you wouldn't be shaking in fear at the sight of me on this ledge, about to fall 750 feet into that fountain below."

"I don't need proof—I believe you. Please," she begged. "I'm trying to understand."

"There are more things in heaven and earth, Clara, than are dreamt of in your philosophy." Before her mind could register the line from *Hamlet*, before she could scream, before she could reach for him, Santino flung himself over the edge.

She felt like it was all a dream, or a nightmare, as she looked down over the railing, down to the fountain below, an exact replica of the Maderno fountain in St. Peter's Square. Tourists were still crawling around the pavement like ants; there was no commotion, no sirens—nothing. "Santino!" she screamed, as if he could hear her.

But he did hear her. He tapped her shoulder, and as she turned around to see him standing inches behind her, a red rose in the ink-stained fingers of his right hand, his designer suit dripping with water, she felt herself fall.

Santino held her in his arms as her eyes opened. "Did I pass out?"

"Indeed. I'm afraid I have that effect on you." He smiled at her. "I caught you. As you witnessed minutes ago, I can move quite quickly."

"You-you jumped! You fell! Oh my God, I'm going to be sick."

"Breathe, sweet angel, breathe."

He held her in silence for several minutes, until she nodded to him and sat up. "Can we go inside?" she asked, glancing toward the ledge that Santino had plunged from.

She sat on his sofa while he changed from the wet suit, gulping rather than sipping her glass of cabernet. *This can't be real,* she thought, *but I saw it!*

"I'm just relieved they cleaned that fountain this morning," Santino said as he emerged from his bedroom in jeans, bare feet, shirtless, and rubbing at his wet hair with a towel.

"I'm relieved you're alive." She shook her head as he sat across from her.

"I can't die, Clara, at least not in any way you can conceive of."

"So you flew?"

"No, I fell, but so quickly the human eye perceived only a faint rush of energy, a breeze possibly."

"The rose..." The red rose sat on the table in front of her.

"A quick detour to the flower shop in the lobby."

"I just can't wrap my mind around it, Santino, it's all so...fantastical."

He reached for her hand and leaned in close. "Now that the theatrics are done, let's slow down a little. Do you have questions?"

"So you're a vampire. That really exists."

"I'd never call us that. We have been made eternal, yes, but we aren't characters in some comic book, Clara—we are real."

"We? There are others?"

"Many others. How many, I do not know. Our *family* consists of a hundred and ten eternals."

"But you can be photographed, you eat, you drink, you...have sex. I mean, shouldn't you like sleep in a coffin or something?"

He laughed and reached for her. She fell against his chest and reveled in the sound of his laughter—he was so rarely openly happy.

Nuzzled against him, she warmed as he spoke against her ear. "Most of those things are myths—made up things born of fantasy and exaggeration. There are a few truths behind those fantasies; at one time, we could not be in the sunlight. We've managed to get around that over time—advances in science, in medicine, have allowed us to overcome those challenges. I'm sure other families have as well to varying degrees. I've seen other eternals, strangers, here in Las Vegas and elsewhere, walking in the sun freely."

"But the blood, then. You don't need blood to survive?"

He didn't answer, and she sensed the subject of blood wasn't something he was eager to speak of.

"I'm just trying to understand," she said, inhaling the scent of him. She'd missed him so much.

"I know, my darling. I want to be open with you; I want you to never doubt me again. These are just things I've never discussed with a mortal—ever."

"I can't believe I'm the first person to ask this stuff." She pulled back to look into his pale eyes.

"I've never interacted with a human who knew *what* I was before."

"Oh," she said, in shock and more than a little joy—*was she special to him?*

"Yes, Clara, you are exquisitely special to me."

"You can read my mind?" The idea made her feel as if she were naked at the Super Bowl.

"Only on rare occasion. I'm not very good at it—I've never been in tune with humans, even when I was one. Nicco excels at that skill, but even he said your mind was strong. The more intelligent the mind, the more opaque it is to us."

"And the blood?"

With a sigh, he grasped her hand and led her back to the sofa.

"I haven't drank blood in twenty-five years. We figured out a way to substitute periodic transfusions rather than feed on humans. Our corporation owns a large medical research facility in Sweden—that is where we get our blood."

"So then why is one of you vampiring on humans?"

He smiled at her. "Vampiring isn't a word."

She relaxed for the first time in a week. He was teasing her again—and despite the heaviness of what she'd just learned, he was next to her and that was enough.

"Who is feeding on the women of Las Vegas then, Santino?" she asked as he reached for her, his hand stroking up her thigh.

"I truly do not know."

"Do you ever want to drink my blood?" she blurted out, wishing she could suck the words back as soon as they were out in the universe.

But Santino wasn't offended. He was aroused. Leaning into her, his lips on her delicate neck, he whispered, "Every moment of every day. I can smell your delicious blood surging through your translucent veins—I can hear it flow. I long to sink my teeth into you and drink, but I never will. We will have to settle for my hungry tongue on your sweet pink pussy."

Her pulse quickened as she felt herself grow wet. She'd been with Santino several times, but she'd never heard him engage in any sort of dirty talk. Despite the shock of the day, she wanted him with a desire she'd never known before.

Santino picked her up, as if she weighed little more than the red rose, and carried her to his bedroom.

* * * * *

"Why me? I mean you can have any woman you want—you've been with other humans, right?" The idea hurt her, but she wasn't naïve enough to think she was unique. They'd made it to his bed, and she was naked—his lips slowly kissed their way up from her instep.

"I love your delicate feet," he said. "And as far as human women, yes, many, thousands I'd say. But Clara—with them, with most of the other humans, it was only sex, nothing more. For you, I can't explain, but it *is* more."

"What about other vampires?" She felt him jolt at the word, so she asked, "I mean other eternals—do you have sex with them? There are women, right?"

His tongue toyed with the back of her knee, that lovely curve from calf to thigh that he adored. "I've never been one to care about gender, but yes, there are females of my kind. We do, yes, but it's different."

His kisses went higher, skating across her inner thigh. Santino was desperate for her, craved the softness of being inside her, but Clara's mind was racing.

"Do we need a condom? Did we ever, or was that—"

"It was for show. I find it easier to just follow the social norms, I suppose. But no, I can't get you pregnant, I will never pass on an STD."

Santino's kisses continued up, past the feminine curve of her hipbone, over the satin skin of her breasts, until he rested at his favorite place, her neck. "I need you, Clara. More than I've ever needed anybody, mortal or not."

Late that night, in the darkness of his room, she rolled over to see him watching her from the end of the bed. "I love to watch you sleep," he said.

"You don't sleep, do you?"

He lay down next to her and pulled her close to him. "Not really, no."

"That's a lot of extra time, I'd love that during finals."

"I read, Shakespeare mostly, or write some but I've never been as good as Will."

"Will?"

"That's a long story."

"Wait, Shakespeare is a vampire? I mean an eternal?"

"No, he's not. I knew him during his lifetime, we were in London then, mostly involved in banking. After he died, he continued to inhabit Southwark."

"Inhabit? Like he's a ghost?"

"I guess you could use that term."

"I don't believe in ghosts."

"But you believe in vampires?" He stroked her back. "You've seen them, ones that even I cannot see. That night in the restaurant, when I drove you home."

"Oh wow," was all she could manage to say. She felt as if a crack in the universe had opened and suddenly she could see through it.

"Clara, there are other things I need to tell you, to explain. I pray that you'll forgive me."

"Santino, it doesn't matter, I—"

"Don't, don't say anything until you've heard what I must tell you. I'm evil—I know now I am of the devil, just like I've been told."

"Don't say that."

Santino listened to her heart beat for a moment before continuing. "I started seeing you, pursuing you, to keep you quiet. What you saw, in the Roman that day—I couldn't risk you telling the police. When my staff foolishly fired you, I was afraid you'd talk. I wanted to keep you close." Santino's face turned even paler than normal. "I couldn't have the Roman linked to those murders."

Clara stared at him, waiting for more, waiting for the unforgivable sin Santino was ready to confess.

"I asked Nicco to romance you, but he refused. He's such a better man than I am, than I ever was."

"Okay, and what else?" she finally said.

"Clara, I used you. I pursued you to keep you quiet!"

She stared into his eyes—for a split second she wondered if it was all fake between them, but she knew it wasn't. "Is that still why we're together then?"

He took a deep breath and fought the urge to touch her. "God no! Clara, you're everything to me. I have a difficult time expressing emotion, with saying the words, but I..." Pink, blood tinged tears filled his eyes; his dark eyelashes blinked them away. "No, it's very real now."

"When did it change?"

"Fully? In San Francisco, that is when I fell hard. But even before that, I began to care for you. It was more than just about the dead body, I swear."

"Why date me to keep me quiet? Why not just kill me?" Clara asked the question in all sincerity, but Santino jumped up as if she'd struck him with a hot iron.

"Is that what you think of me? That I'm a *monster*?"

She rose up next to him, desperate to save them. "I didn't mean it like that. I'm sorry, please, I'm struggling to understand."

"Once, when I had to, I fed on humans. Yes, a couple of times by mistake I've-I've taken lives. We fed on the infirm, the evil, the hopeless, and even more reprehensible maybe, those who sought the curiosity of it. But I only fed on those who *wanted* it, Clara. I'm not a murderer."

Clara felt warm, hopeful. "Is that the worst of it, Santino? That you originally showed interest in me to see what I knew, to keep me quiet?"

"I drugged you. That day in the restaurant—do you remember Reginald the waiter?"

"Yes, I remember."

"He's not a waiter. He's one of us. I had him slip a drug into your water."

"Why?"

"I can't read your mind, angel. I mean, barely. The stronger the mind, the harder to read. And you, my God, you're brilliant. I wanted to see what you really thought of the body—so we gave you a hallucinogenic to make it easier."

"But?"

"But you had a horrible reaction to it, it made you sick. That was *never* my intention, I swear."

Clara leaned back into the plush pillows.

"Is there more?" she asked.

Santino sat next to her and stared at his hands. "No, those are my sins. I am so sorry. Please don't leave me, Clara. I *need* you."

"I'm not going anywhere. You may struggle with the words, but I don't. I love you, Santino Marchetti. And however it happened, I'm glad it did. When I'm with you, I'm alive."

Santino took her into his arms—he'd never been happier, not as a mortal man, and not as an eternal. His Clara, his perfect angel, she forgave him his sins.

Ten

Landon caught her one afternoon grabbing clean clothes from her drawer. "Oh wait, is that my long lost former best friend Clara Marie Denton I hear? Or is it Mrs. Marchetti now?" He popped his head into her room and smiled wide at her.

"I'm sorry—it's been crazy. Ever since that night we've just been inseparable."

"Well text a guy back once in a while, baby girl. I worry and stuff."

"No need," she answered, searching for a pair of shoes. "I'm in love with him, Landon."

"Be careful, Clara Belle, okay? I mean I'm sure he's great but he's like a gazillionaire and you're a college student—a maid in his hotel. Have a great time with him, get what you can, but don't hang your hat on forever with this one."

She shook her head at him. "I know how it looks, but this is real. He loves me."

"Did he say that?"

"Well, no, but he does. I just know it."

Landon nodded—he knew she was too far gone to get her to slow down now. "Have you seen that blond blog guy?"

Clara shook her head. "No, he's messaged me a few times. Oh but hey, I have more good news. My mom is doing great this time in rehab—they've given her a job there at the center. That's never happened before."

Landon sat down on her bed. "She may just surprise you, Clara Belle."

Clara smiled. "She may just. Hey, I've got to go—come out to the Roman soon, have dinner on us."

"Now you're an *us*," he said with snort.

The truth was, she'd been avoiding Matthew. How could she face him now, knowing what she knew about Santino? But her efforts to avoid Matthew didn't last long. As she pulled into Santino's private parking area, she was shocked to see Matthew's beat-up truck. She pulled her own beater next to his and watched as her security detail, now with even more guards, drove past her to wait for her to leave the Roman.

She glanced up at the cameras—she knew Santino would be watching.

"Hey stranger," Matthew said as he opened her car door.

"Um, oh hi. What are you doing here?" *How did you get to this private area,* was more what she meant. The love of her life was a vampire, and here stood her friend, a vampire hunter.

"I know what you're thinking, and I know you're still seeing him. It's okay, Clara, I'm here for you and Vittoria."

"Vittoria? Huh?"

"I told you I've been seeing her. She lives in the suites—that's why I'm parked here—she lets me."

Clara leaned against his truck bed—thoroughly confused. In her pocket, her phone buzzed with a text, and then a phone call. She knew it was Santino, and her time with Matthew would be limited. If she didn't answer, he'd show up.

"Wait, you're *really* hooking up with Vittoria, his assistant?"

He nodded. "Yeah, I know, right? It's totally nuts—but she seems to dig me. She's so different, Clara, I just can't seem to think straight when I'm around her."

The irony, Clara thought. No one had ever told her that Vittoria was an eternal, but to Clara, all the signs were there. She only hoped that Matthew wasn't in danger—he really was a decent guy.

"Listen, Matthew, be careful around here, okay? I mean, keep your ideas on the down-low, if you know what I mean."

He nodded. "Got it, but hey, don't avoid me. You're one of the few friends I have in Vegas. Sorry I had to break your heart."

"Uh, what?" she said incredulously.

"I'm kidding!"

She shot him a wink. "I'm heading up—let's catch up soon, okay?"

Upstairs, Santino was pacing. When Clara came out of the elevator, he was at the door. "I know, Santino, I know. Don't be mad," she said as she dropped her bag on his counter.

"I'm not mad at you, my angel. I'm angry with my rebellious assistant. Did that pest bother you?" He took her into his arms.

"No. He's a sweet guy; it's just awkward. When I met him, I thought he was nuts, and now, I mean, he's not nuts right? You are what he says."

"I guess technically. But Clara, he wants to eliminate my kind—to hunt us."

"I don't think the Hunter thing is literal—he wants to know about you, that's all."

Santino shook his head. "This is an age-old battle, my angel, one of many that you couldn't understand. Please trust me."

That night in bed, something changed between them. They'd grown closer each day, and that night, as she slid a finger inside him at the pinnacle of his ecstasy, his teeth sank into her neck.

As her sweet blood flowed onto his tongue, he knew he'd passed the point of no return with Clara—she'd wrapped around his heart, and there was no going back. He had to have her—forever.

They came together in a thrash—and later, as he healed the slight bleeding at her throat with his own blood, she looked into his eyes. "That meant something, right?" she asked.

"I got carried away," was all he managed to say.

"Santino, you're everything to me," she said sleepily as he held her all night long.

The next day, he confronted Vittoria—she'd gone too far with the Hunter.

"What do you want me to say, Vittoria? That's it's fine? I can't do that. Or maybe you want me to punish you, like I did your father? I can't do that either." Santino watched as pink-tinged tears worked their way down her cheeks.

"You are the one who asked me to see him," she argued.

"I asked you to keep an eye on him, not fuck him! Not bring him into my home!" He slammed his fist onto her desk.

"Do you think I planned this? To have feelings for him? After what I went through before? After what we did to them?"

He sat down across from her. She was right. "I know, Vittoria. What are we going to do?"

She sat down next to him, her hand on his. "Santino, do something. Tell me to leave him, or tell me to take him and go—please don't leave this to me. Don't let Matthew end up like Howard..."

"We didn't do that to him," Santino said quietly.

"I could love him," was all she could say. "Would you be willing to meet him? See what you think? Please, for me? And for Clara."

"I'll think about it, Vittoria. That's the best I can do for now."

"Can it ever last, do you think?"

"Love? No, I don't think so. But, I confess that even my frozen heart hopes that maybe it could."

* * * * *

The next afternoon, she got a call from Santino. "I'm going to meet this Hunter so both of you will let it rest once and for all," he'd said. "But I'm not leaving the Roman."

"Fair enough," Clara said.

She was once again low on gas, so she asked Matthew to pick her up on his way to the Roman. Santino sent a car, as usual, but she ignored it—she wanted to talk to Matthew *before* he met Santino.

"I can't believe I'm going to meet a vampire," he said, his hand shaking as he shifted.

"Matthew, please don't talk like that."

"You know, I didn't believe any of it either until I was a teenager, actually," Matthew said as he navigated the heavy afternoon traffic from campus toward the Strip.

"So what changed that?" Clara asked.

"I saw a ghost," he answered.

"How did you know that it was a ghost? I guess I still don't believe they exist," she said, although her mind wandered back to the underground restaurant.

"They exist, whether you believe it or not, Clara." He shifted lanes and looked in his rearview mirror. "That black car is still following us."

"I know. I'm hoping it's from Santino and not the police. I asked him, and he never really gave me a clear answer. He's good at that."

"Do you need to stop home and change?" He glanced down to her shorts and flip-flops.

"No, I have clothes in his penthouse."

Matthew bit his lower lip, determined not to say anything, but couldn't bring himself to stay silent. "Clara, I know he looks like this great guy to you, handsome, rich, all of that. But please never forget that he is a killer—literally, a cold-blooded killer. I don't know enough about this group of paranormals yet to know how they operate, but he could hurt you, kill you."

"He would never do that."

"But you'll be cautious? That's all I ask."

"I promise," she said to calm him down. "Tell me more about the ghost."

"Well, it was when we lived in Sacramento. My mom was a nurse—she worked in the cancer center. One afternoon I was sitting in the hallway near the nurse's station—we were going to meet my dad for dinner—and as she finished up some paperwork, I saw a man die."

"Alright, that's horrible, but..."

"Clara, I watched his soul rise from his body, move through the ward, and drift down the hallway in front of me. No one else saw it but me."

"Matthew, are you sure that..."

"I know what I saw, what I felt. In that moment, I knew that there were things in this world that we don't see, that we don't have awareness of, that don't fit into the rules of *real* that we make up for ourselves. If souls leave bodies, then maybe my father wasn't so crazy after all."

"So you went from the glimpse of a soul to vampires?"

"Dad was mostly interested in blood drinkers. He didn't use the term vampire—he found that to be a false twist on the mythology of blood drinkers—a false combining of their story with Vlad the Impaler in Romania. Anyway, to make a long story short, he became aware of this group of them in Vegas, and here we are. He even met Santino's father once."

Matthew turned toward the parking garage and the black car stopped around the block. "They aren't following us into the garage," he said, glancing back.

"No, they don't. I think because we're on camera—he can see me."

* * * * *

"I have no idea why I'm doing this," Santino said as he pulled his tie off that evening.

"Because it seems to mean a lot to Vittoria." Clara stood teetering on her new stilettos at his long mirror and slathered on lipgloss. "And he's my friend."

"His mission in life is to do me harm, you realize that right?"

"Because he doesn't get it—but this could be a good thing. Matthew isn't a bad guy, and he's promised to be civil tonight." Clara leaned into the mirror. "I can't find my earrings; I'm sure I put them here before I took a shower."

"Odd," he said with an eyebrow raise. "And as far as the Hunter, I am mostly just glad he is no longer pursuing you."

"He was never pursuing me, Santino."

"You kissed him, more than once, my angel. Do you know what that did to me?"

She turned to him—she had no idea then that he would ever find out. But now, she knew that Santino wasn't the type of being you hid things from easily. "I'm sorry about that. Honestly we had no chemistry—and he's bonkers over your sexy assistant."

Santino nodded. "Ah yes, the Vittoria problem."

Clara walked toward him and placed her hands on his chest. "Let them have their fun. He's harmless, I promise you."

"That's unfortunate for him, because Vittoria is the opposite of harmless. She will chew him up and spit him out—and it won't be the first time."

He glanced at his watch. "Let me change, darling, they're supposed to meet us here in a few minutes. I still do not understand why I've been asked to *dress down* for dinner."

"It's casual, that's why. Now, where are my earrings?"

"I might have them," he said with a rare smile. He reached over to his jacket, slung over a chair, and pulled out a small velvet box.

"What's that?" she asked in shock.

"Earrings." He held the box out to her.

She took the box and stared at it. "A gift? Why?" She'd never had a boyfriend who bought her more than a ten-dollar bottle of drugstore perfume, and even then, it was always with strings attached.

"Because I adore you, and because, Clara, these will be brilliant on your perfect ears. Now open it."

As she popped open the box, a pair of diamond stud earrings glittered in the light of Santino's bathroom. She'd never seen anything so beautiful—or expensive. In a rush of emotion, she flung herself toward him. Except, she forgot she wasn't in flats, and the four-inch stiletto heels gave way against the terrazzo tile floor.

She screamed as her head missed the marble countertop by inches, smashing into the mirror and cracking it.

He reached for her, desperate to break her fall, but was seconds too late. Blood ran from her forehead, down her face, onto her neck, and finally across her new white dress. His focus on Clara, he didn't notice the intruder until it was too late.

Matthew Hunter lunged at Santino, the weapon plunging into Santino's heart.

The blond man, the Hunter, stood in front of him, his hand shaking at the end of a long spike. Clara, bloody and injured, screamed again as Santino fell to the ground.

"I had to," Matthew muttered, backing away in horror as Santino gyrated on the tile floor. Clara, blood still flowing from the cut on her forehead, was on top of Santino, panicked, horrified. Her love was dying, right in front of her.

Vittoria appeared in the doorway, looking from Santino on the floor to Matthew, who was white, hunched against the wall in shock at what he'd done.

"You idiot," she said to Matthew. She walked over and sat on the floor next to him, her hand on his knee.

"What? I-a stake through the heart! Vittoria, he's a vampire. He was trying to murder Clara!" Vittoria shook her head and looked toward Clara.

"Are you okay, you're bleeding," she said to Clara, reaching for a washcloth to wipe the blood off her face.

"I'm fine, it's just, I fell, cut myself on the mirror—but save him, call 911, Santino is dying!"

Santino rose up, angry but very much alive. "I'm going to kill you, mother fucker," he said to Matthew with a growl. His right hand grabbed the end of the stake and pulled it from his chest.

Clara stared at the stake as it clinked across the floor. There was no blood on it, or on Santino's chest. She watched as the opening it had come from sealed up, only a long tear in his tailored shirt showing any evidence of what Matthew had done.

"But a stake through the heart is—"

"Just a myth, I'm afraid," Vittoria answered. "Come, my blond hunk of hotness, because I fear Santino the Eternal is about to do you great bodily harm."

* * * * *

Matthew sat on the sofa next to Vittoria, her hand in his. "Your hands are always cold," he said to break the nervous silence.

"Cold hands, cold heart," she teased.

"Your boss really *is* a vampire—and you knew." Matthew had fallen hard for her, but he couldn't reconcile the fact that she'd kept the truth from him.

"Yes, but he's not a killer, Matthew. He's a good man—things have changed. Your perception of what he is has been skewed by folklore."

"I can't believe it's real. I mean all this time, I sought the truth, I believed it, but now—I can't believe it's not all fantasy." Matthew thought of his myriad of followers waiting for news on his meeting that evening with a true vampire, and he realized that there was no way this secret could ever leave this penthouse. *People don't want to know, they want to wonder,* he thought.

"Is he going to kill me?" he asked, fighting the fear that threatened to overtake him. If he had to die, meeting the very thing he'd sought his entire life wouldn't be the worst way to go.

"No, he's just a little pissed that you shoved a stake into his heart, I think," she said with a giggle.

"While you were in the powder room I heard her scream. I ran in, and I saw him over her, blood flowing from her. I reacted."

"He loves her. He hasn't said it yet—he's never professed that kind of love to *anyone*—but he does and would never harm her. But, my resourceful lover, where did you get the stake from?"

"It's always in my messenger bag. I've carried it for years." He looked down—the leather bag was still slung across his body.

"Do you have a silver bullet in there too?" Santino asked from the doorway.

"I-I," Matthew stammered. He knew he was in trouble—but the importance of having a real eternal that near to him was more than he could fathom. "I might," he finally answered.

Santino laughed, frightening Matthew even more.

Reaching down to button his new shirt, Santino said, "That wasn't very nice, Mr. Hunter." He walked to the bar and poured a tumbler of scotch.

"I'm sorry. I thought you were harming Clara."

"I would *never* harm Clara," Santino seethed, turning toward the couple on the couch. "But why should I not harm *you*?"

"Because he's mine, Santino. You owe me that," Vittoria said, rising from the couch and walking toward him.

"I won't tell anyone," Matthew said, gauging the distance to the door in case he needed to run.

"Tell whomever you like—blast it all over all of those social media sites filled with others as crazy as you are. You are just like your nutcase father."

"My father? You know him?" Matthew began to think back to the vampires his father hunted so long ago. A sudden revelation struck him. "That's right! My father was on the trail of your father decades ago."

Santino smiled at the weakness of the human brain—even one as spectacular as Matthew Hunter's. "That was me. My father, my grandfather, my great-grandfather—all me through the ages."

"You tried to kill him! You drank his blood, but he escaped."

"Lies," Santino said flatly. With a long sip of his drink, he added, "Your father liked to embellish."

Matthew sensed Santino was telling the truth—he had no reason to lie.

"What happened?"

"Would you like a drink?" Santino asked, refilling his own empty tumbler with the amber scotch.

"Uh, Bud Light?" Matthew answered—he had never been one to drink much else.

Santino cringed, shook his head, and walked over and sat across from Matthew. "Listen, you seem a little smarter, and a lot braver, than your father. He was in the same room with me, once. He held some mirror up to my face, then wet himself, dropped it, and ran. But Vittoria means a lot to me, and she seems to be attached to you. And Clara is fond of you—so go about your business. Stay clear of me and we're good."

"But a blood drinker is loose in Las Vegas—I can't walk away from that." Matthew felt Vittoria's grasp on his thigh.

"Drop it, Hunter, or you could find yourself quite uncomfortable."

Eleven

"**B**ut we never go out," Clara whined the next night in his penthouse.

Santino stood in front of the mirror in his dressing room straightening his tie as she stood in the doorway pouting.

"Nonsense, darling. I'm taking you out tonight."

"Away from the Roman? Around people, in public?" she argued.

He let the tie fall and walked toward her. "You look ravishing," he said, admiring her figure in the tight maroon sheath dress he'd sent to her apartment that afternoon.

"Thank you for the dress," she said as she let him take her into his arms.

"The shoes?"

"I couldn't walk in them—I'm sorry." Landon tried and tried to help her balance on the sky-high Louboutin heels, but she couldn't get the hang of it.

He glanced down at her delicate feet in her leather ballet flats—the nicest pair of shoes in her pre-Santino wardrobe. "Do not worry, my angel, you look beautiful as you are. We can't have you injuring yourself again, after all."

"I'm sorry I was whining. I can be an ungrateful witch."

"Please don't use that word. No, you are young, and you wish to go out on the town. You have no need for apologies. It is I who am sorry. Where would you like to dine tonight, sweet Clara?"

She cocked her head to the side and gave it some thought. "There's that one place way up on the top of the Strat—doesn't it spin or something?"

He looked into her eyes. The pull she had on him was so strong, he felt like he might burst. "Well, the Stratosphere Tower, that is certainly an option I hadn't thought of," he teased, rubbing his nose against hers.

"Is it gross?" She'd never even been to the top of the iconic tower—the twenty-dollar cost of admission was always out of her range just for a trip up.

Santino shrugged his shoulders. "I wouldn't know, but if that is what my angel would like, that is precisely where we will go."

As they left his penthouse, Santino brushed away the nerves at going out in public in an uncontrolled environment. He purposefully kept a low profile around town, but he wanted to do this for her.

When he texted Vittoria the change in plans, and would she please secure the best table at the Top of the World restaurant, she nearly dropped her phone.

When he told his driver to please bring the car around, they were headed to the Stratosphere for dinner, the driver nearly ran into a pole.

But Clara was thrilled. Her senior year in high school all of the kids went there before prom and then plastered their happy pics all over Facebook. She'd cried herself to sleep that night looking at them. She'd been asked to prom, by a boy she liked, but didn't have the money for the dress. He ended up going out with a girl she hated, Donna Metzger, the resident mean girl.

But now, she was in a designer dress, something Italian but she couldn't remember the brand name, and she was with her Prince Charming. No, she wouldn't post a picture of Santino to social media, but she could live with that.

"I'm sorry about the shoes," she said for the third time that night. "I'll send them back—I only tried them on the carpet, you can get your money back."

He pulled her close and slid his hand up her bare leg. "I don't care about the shoes, angel. Keep them, or sell them if you'd like. I wanted to spoil you a little, nothing more. I desperately want you to be you, my darling, I have no desire to change you."

"I love the dress," she said before kissing him hard on the lips. "It gives me curves I don't really have."

"Oh you have curves, my girl. In fact later I intend to run my tongue along every inch of those dangerous curves."

* * * * *

"Oh an escalator, how efficient," Santino said with a sneer as he took Clara's hand to lead her up from the casino floor toward the tower. The place was loud and congested, and more alarmingly to him, garish.

"I can't believe in all the years you've lived here, you've never been inside the Strat," she said as they stepped off the escalator and made their way past a crowded food court toward the elevators.

"I remember when this monstrosity was built," he said looking around the shopping mall-like atmosphere.

"Oh, don't be so upscale all the time. It's fun, and what would the Vegas skyline be without it?"

"Classy?" he said with a rare laugh.

"This restaurant is super fancy, though. Thanks for bringing me—I feel like a princess."

He pulled her toward the elevators. "Let's get you up to your tower, Princess Clara."

* * * * *

"Oh my God it really does spin!" she said as the hostess led them to their table against the windows.

"Indeed, it does seem to revolve," Santino said as he reached for the wine list. "These vintages are abysmal." He put the folder back, determined to score a better bottle, even if he had to have Vittoria bring it over from the Roman.

"You're raining on my parade," she said, reaching for his hand.

"You are right, my lovely. I am with *you*, and that makes this a splendid place to be."

After Santino was able to negotiate a bottle of cabernet he would drink with the sommelier, Clara relaxed.

"Can we go hang out on the observation deck after dinner? The guy at the front said we could for free."

Santino took a sip of the wine. "My darling you worry a lot over money, don't you?"

"I've always had to, I guess. When I leave school, I'll be broke. I have a decent scholarship, but all of the other expenses are burying me under. I'm not complaining though—I'm the first one from my family to even attend college."

Santino knew in that moment that no matter what happened between them, her education expenses would be fully paid by his corporation when she graduated. "I have more money than I know what to do with, my sweet angel. I'm honored to spend it on you. And yes, we'll spend all the time you'd like on that cold, windy observation deck."

"You'll just have to keep me warm," she flirted, finding his foot with hers.

Halfway through dinner, salmon for Santino and steak for Clara, it happened. His world revolved as the restaurant did.

Clara looked up as the elderly woman stopped at their table, her face flush, her gnarled hands bracing for balance against the table as she stared at them.

"Santino," she blurted out.

Clara looked at him—his normally stoic demeanor gave way to panic.

"No," he snapped, "I'm sorry. What?"

Clara knew he was shaken by the old woman. She steadied herself before looking down at the plain gold band on her finger. "Oh, young man, I'm sorry. You look exactly, I mean exactly, like a man from my younger days. I apologize for disturbing you."

"It was no disturbance, ma'am," Santino said, his voice shaky.

The woman returned to her table, but continued to glance over at them in confusion for the rest of their nearly silent meal. Finally, Clara couldn't take the tension anymore. "Did you love her?"

His eyes snapped toward hers. "No," he said. "I've never loved a mortal before. But I cared for her. With Esther, I let it go too far. It was during the mid-fifties, she was a showgirl at the Dunes. We became close when Sinatra was doing shows there. Esther fell hard and fast for me, sadly."

"So you had a relationship with her?" Clara asked, her mind still wandering to the words he'd said moments prior—that he'd never loved a mortal *before*. Did he mean before *her*?

"Yes, but she didn't mean as much to me as I meant to her, I'm not proud to say."

Clara's eyes met his. She had to ask. "Do I mean anything more to you?"

He took her hands in his. "You know you do, my angel. That's why this is so very hard! Look at her, Clara, and look at me. Can you see why I keep my distance? Why you and I present problems I just can't wrap my mind around?"

"I will grow old, and you won't. But if someday you love me enough, maybe it won't matter?"

"My innocent angel, life and love do not work that way."

After dinner, they made their way to the elevators that led them up to the top of the tower. Clara leaned against the railing as the wind whipped around her. The chill in the air at over 800 feet seemed to mock the chill between them after the appearance of Esther into their lives.

Clara looked out over the glimmering lights of the city, the reality of what she thought was a fairy tale descending on her. She looked back when he put his jacket over her bare shoulders. "Please, my darling, you'll get ill," he said, with words so full of meaning she couldn't bear it. *Ill and old,* she thought.

On the ride back to the Roman, they sat in silence. With a squeeze of her hand, he made his decision—one that made him feel happier than he'd ever felt. He'd decided—Clara would not be Esther, she would not age.

He leaned over to kiss her—his Clara would be his, forever.

In a rush of emotion, he carried her from the car to his bed. What happened with Esther was done, he couldn't take any of it back. But Clara, *that* he could do differently.

"Are you mine, angel?" He unzipped her dress—he needed her naked.

"Always," she answered.

"Always," he repeated as his lips found her neck.

His fingers slid inside her as he kissed her lips, alive with warmth for the last time. Clara had to die tonight so that they may live.

"So sweet, so wet." He drew his fingers from her and licked each one slowly, one by one while she watched. "That part will never change, my darling."

"Please don't tease me tonight—I'm dying for you," she moaned.

"Yes, you will." He nipped at her lip with his sharp teeth—just enough to taste her blood before he went lower. Clara thrashed as his tongue explored her, all of her, worshipping her in places no one had ever touched. Tonight he would claim her, every inch of her, before her body was transformed.

He sank his tongue in deep as she tightened around him. His fingers wrapped around her clitoris, and with a slight squeeze, he let her come for the first time.

"More?" he asked as her eyelids fluttered open.

"I need to feel you." She reached for him, desperate to feel his weight on top of her.

He plunged into her as his teeth found his favorite place on her neck, the place he would soon rip open as he drained her.

She clenched around him, coming again, and yet again as he thrust into her, and when she was exhausted, he allowed himself to have his own climax, allowing himself only a shallow bite against her neck...for now.

Her palm brushed against his chest as she fought sleep to talk to him. The sex before had been more intense, more emotional, than any they'd ever shared.

"You bit me again," she said sleepily, her fingers dancing over his nipples.

"I got carried away," he said, the taste of her blood still dancing across his palate.

She dozed off but he nudged her awake. "Clara, I want you to be with me forever."

"I want that," she answered with a yawn. His stamina was exhausting.

"Tonight you shall be made eternal."

Suddenly she was awake. She sprang up and looked at him. "Santino, no, what?"

He licked his lips—he could still taste her as his joy turned to anger.

"You said always, you said forever."

"I didn't realize you were being literal."

"I see. To you, those were just figures of speech, phrases...lies."

"We've only just begun," she said, reaching for him, but he pushed her away.

"I can't watch you grow old and die, Clara. I'm not that strong."

"I'm so young—we have a long time to make that decision. Can't we just live in the now?"

"In the now," he said. "To me, my angel, your lifespan is like that of when you had a pet goldfish as a child."

"Santino, I want to be with you, forever, I mean that. I'm just not ready to be made eternal tonight. I'm asking for a little more time."

"You're right," he said, lying back down and turning away from her. "I should have known better." Bitterness flooded him as she fell asleep—there'd been a crucial flaw in his plan. They could live forever, but their love could not.

* * * * *

"I can't watch her die," Santino said to Vittoria the next morning.

She sat down on the sofa in his office and sipped her latte. "Not wanting to be made eternal at twenty-one is a long way from dying, my prince."

"I have to be strong enough for all of us. I need you to trust me, and most importantly, obey me."

"All of us?"

"You can't continue with Matthew Hunter."

Vittoria stood up and glared at him. "Santino, please, just give me a little more time with him." She wouldn't lose Matthew over Santino's crisis of faith, she couldn't.

He understood the pain he was causing them both—but he knew what he had to do. "Clara needs to grow old then, if that is her choice. Get married, have children, age, and yes, die. And she has to live this short life far away from me. Believe me, I'd give up eternity in a heartbeat if I could share in that—it would be worth it all just to live one lifetime with her."

"There has to be a better way—this is cruel, my prince. It nearly destroyed Esther."

"Life is cruel, you know that. She has to leave me."

Vittoria took a deep breath. "So it's you and me, then? For eternity?"

*****

Clara hummed as she cleaned her rooms the next day at the Roman. The night before, Santino wanted to make her one of them—he wanted her to live forever. Forever with him—the thought thrilled her. He did love her; she knew it.

Clara knew he'd been hurt when she refused, but she would make him understand that a little more time was all she was asking for. Time to finish school, time to get a job on her own for the first time, and maybe the chance to experience her twenties with him at her side. "Maybe when I'm twenty-nine," she said out loud as she fluffed the pillows. He'd be over-protective, no doubt about that, she reasoned, but it would work out—their love would last.

She left the room and walked toward the changing area—she was anxious to get home and get ready for dinner that night with Santino. She'd planned to tell him that she wanted to live forever, with him, if he could just agree to a few more years.

Her supervisor turned the corner and stopped in front of her. *Even she can't bring me down today,* Clara thought. *He loves me.*

"Clara, I need you to do me a favor. I know you're about to clock out, but Juana went home sick suddenly and I need suite 17809 cleaned. It's vacant and I need it turned quickly for a VIP."

"Oh sure," Clara said with a smile, hoping she could win a little favor with Ms. Lopez.

Upstairs, Clara stuck her key card in the door and opened it. She didn't bother with knocking—Ms. Lopez said the room was vacant, and she was in a hurry.

"No, no, NO!" Clara heard her own voice scream, but it was as if the sound were coming from someone else, not from her. This couldn't be happening to *her.* He wouldn't do that to her—he loved her.

"Clara!" Santino yelled, jumping off the naked woman and turning to her.

Her eyes went from the naked Santino to the woman on the bed. Her large breasts were smeared with blood, her dark hair fanned out over the pillow.

"Tell her, Santino," Vittoria said as Clara stared. "Tell her!"

She wanted to run, but was frozen. "I can explain," he said as he reached for his pants.

"It's okay, little human—I'm his wife." Vittoria sat up and leveled her eyes at Clara.

"Wife," Clara repeated, struggling not to pass out. The room was swirling.

She tried to look at Santino, but he wouldn't make eye contact. "You should go," he said, turning his back to her.

"Please, I don't know what this is, but I love you. You love me! I know you do. Santino, I'll go with you, I'll be made eternal. Take me now, I swear I want this."

The room was silent. He could hear Clara's heart pounding. This wasn't supposed to happen this way—she wasn't following the script. The pain emanating from her was nearly unbearable as he said the final words. "You had your chance, Clara, you made your choice and it wasn't me. Go live your life—this is done."

* * * * *

He couldn't move. Santino sat in the dark hotel suite until he'd smoked through his pack of cigarettes.

"You should get dressed," Vittoria said from the corner of the room.

"Why? Who cares?"

"I do. It reminds me of what we did, it sickens me, Santino."

"We had to—we had to with Esther and Howard, and we had to with Clara."

Vittoria walked toward him and tossed his pants on his lap. "No, it's wrong. Maybe we shouldn't have let them fall in love with us, but they did. The damage was already done—all we did is hurt them more. Did you see her eyes, Santino?"

"Yes!" he screamed, standing up. "Do you think I wanted that? Any of this?"

"No, my prince, but you hide behind not wanting to hurt her. You've already hurt her—what you are really running from is loving her."

Santino got dressed, and as he reached into his pocket for his buzzing phone, he blocked Clara Denton. "It's done, it's over. She didn't even question it. Once again, she just believed the worst about me."

"That's what you wanted," Vittoria snapped.

"I know; it had to be. But I guess in the back of my mind somewhere I thought she wouldn't go, I thought she'd believe in me, in us."

"Go talk to her, Santino. Take a chance on love, for once."

"I cannot," he said as he walked out the door.

Twelve

It happened that very night. Clara went to bed sobbing, her heart aching for Santino, her mind replaying the sight of him having sex with Vittoria, *his wife*, over and over. She'd tried to call him, but her number had been blocked. Matthew wouldn't even answer her desperate texts.

What she didn't know was that the monster had been there the entire day, waiting in her nearly empty closet. He waited until her roommate left for his job waiting tables until late in the night; he waited until Clara finished her infernal sobbing. When the girl, not his normal type at all, finally drifted into a fitful sleep, he slipped from the closet and stood over her bed.

The killer liked blondes, curvy ones, and this mousy haired, built-like-a-boy being didn't arouse him in the slightest. *It's not about pleasure this time,* he reminded himself. *This time, it's about taking what is Santino's.*

"You ignored my other gifts, Santino," he said aloud. "But this time, you will hurt as I have all these years."

This wasn't a killing he would savor. The girl repulsed him—she smelled like Santino, the one he hated the most. The monster couldn't kill Santino, but he could tarnish everything that he loved: his city, his beloved hotel, and now, the stupid human that Santino loved.

The monster knew that the connection to the killings alone would be enough to force the family to move on, to reinvent themselves as they'd done so many times in the past. And this time, the monster would be among them once again. Santino would be exiled—Santino the killer of humans in Las Vegas during the modern age. The family could never allow him to remain in power, to lead the family toward the future. *Santino Marchetti has returned to the old ways,* they'd chatter in horror. The monster smiled.

When the monster sank his teeth into her neck, Clara felt pain. The sharp bite jolted her awake, but she couldn't move. His strong hands held her still as he tore the gash wider, deeper, to allow her blood to flow into him. For Clara, the pain only lasted for a minute—then she simply felt numb. Her hands dropped from around her assailant's wrists—she no longer had the strength to fight. Then she heard him—not in the room, but from somewhere inside of her soul. "Clara, are you in danger?" the voice asked. *Santino!*

"Help," she pleaded out loud into the room in a voice so faint, even the monster draining her of her blood didn't hear it. Her eyelids fluttered open—the man killing her was on top of her; he'd been sucking her blood slowly, as if he were savoring the moments before he took her brief life, but now he looked at her. *I won't even get to see my killer,* she thought absently as she looked at him, his face covered with a leather hood, only his eyes and his lips exposed. His red-tinged pale eyes stared at her vacantly.

"He can't save you," the monster said, his accent thick, his voice raspy and hoarse.

He leaned in to finish the job, to drain her. Once again, she heard *him,* just as her eyes closed. "Clara, hold on," Santino said to her—she knew occasionally he could read her mind, but she never knew she could read his.

The pain returned as the monster's teeth left her flesh. It burned like fire as the warm blood gushed down her chest, soaking her worn nightshirt. The last thing Clara saw before she lost consciousness was Vittoria pulling the hooded being from her. The thing turned to fight Vittoria, but instead, for some reason, decided to run.

"Clara, hang on, Santino's less than a minute away." Clara was confused, and dizzier than she'd ever been. *Was she dead?* Her eyes closed as Vittoria, with sharp teeth, tore into her own wrist and forced it onto Clara's mouth. "Drink!" she snapped as the metallic, viscous fluid flowed down Clara's throat.

* * * * *

When she woke up, everything hurt. There were tubes poking into the veins in her arm, and her neck was bandaged, the tape pulled her skin as she turned her head to see him. The dark, brooding figure of Santino was beside her in a chair—his eyes were closed.

Clara wasn't in a hospital, despite the medical machines surrounding her. It wasn't Santino's penthouse either—the room was old, like a historic mansion possibly. She tried to remember what happened, but it was all fuzzy.

"You're awake, my angel," he said, his light eyes studying her.

"Where am I?"

"Rome. My home. I grew up here, in this palace."

"How did I get here?"

"I flew you here."

"You can fly?"

His lips curled into a smile, and he relaxed for the first time in days, for the first time since the monster had come to take his Clara.

"On a jet, my love, rather than Superman-style."

"Oh. This," she said, pointing to the bag of blood flowing into her arm, "am I? Vittoria gave me blood."

"As have I—my blood is far stronger than hers. But she saved your life that night. I have no idea *why* she was there, but I'm glad that she was."

"If I lost blood, and the two of you fed me blood, does that mean I'm a vampire?"

He cringed. "There's that word again. No, darling, you are not. You didn't lose that much blood. We've merely fortified you—you should have one hell of an immune system after this though."

"I'll be okay?"

"You'll be okay."

"And us, Santino? Is there even an *us*?"

He reached for her hand. "There is an us, Clara. I just don't know what that future looks like. I do know I failed at sending you away."

"I knew you set it up—for me to clean that room, to see you with her."

"I didn't do anything with her, you are correct. That rouse has worked in the past, but you, Clara, didn't let go quite as I'd planned. I wanted to save you from *me*, my darling."

"Love doesn't die that easily, Santino."

He looked at her—his love; he'd never have the strength to be away from her again.

Her mind drifted to that horrible day. "You're married to Vittoria?" The very thought caused her stomach to lurch.

"No. I was, briefly, and it didn't work out."

There was a loud beep from one of the machines attached to Clara and Santino jolted.

A woman rushed into the room and checked the machine as Santino nervously paced. She replaced a needle in Clara's arm, spoke to Santino in hurried Italian, and then left the room.

"Loose line, nothing wrong," he said as the door closed.

"Why did the killer come for me?"

He looked over at her and sat back down, pulling the chair closer so he could hold her hand. "To frame me. Possibly to hurt me, I don't know."

"But how would he know about me?"

"Clara, the killer, I came to realize, is preying on women that I have been sexually involved with."

"But there have been nine women—"

"Yes," he said, leaning down to kiss her hand.

"Oh," was all she could manage to say, the jealousy surging like a fever. Then an even more stomach-turning thought struck her. "Vittoria, I mean, you've, you and she... But that night, he put up no fight when she saved me. It was as if he knew her."

"Clara, Vittoria and I were briefly married as humans, here in Rome, to create a family alliance. There's been nothing romantic between us. As far as the killer knowing her, I'm sure he does. I fear he is one of the family—one of us."

She was in love with a vampire, and attacked by another vampire, and saved by his ex-wife the vampire. Her mind struggled to make sense of it all, but he was hers again, and that was what mattered most.

* * * * *

"Are you ever going to tell me about Esther? Seeing her—that was what tore us apart." Clara had healed quickly in Santino's palace over the previous week, but she had to know his past so she could better navigate their future.

"If we must," he sighed. "It was the 1950s. We hadn't been in the new city for long when we fell in with the entertainment crowd."

"Where were you before Vegas?" Clara asked.

"San Francisco, and New Orleans before that. Some of our family remained in New Orleans."

"Vampires in New Orleans—why doesn't that surprise me," Clara said with the shake of her head.

"Some fiction is based on fact, my angel."

"And Esther?"

"Vittoria fell madly in love with an eccentric named Howard Hughes." Santino leaned back in his chair and waited for Clara to absorb the details.

"*The* Howard Hughes? The germophobe? The insane guy who let his fingernails grow all long and..."

"Some of that is untrue. But then, he was a handsome young inventor, and Vittoria was in love with him. That was about the same time as I met Esther."

"So you did love her?" Clara asked jealously.

"No, but I did care for her, however, and it ended badly."

"Okay, so in the fifties, before I was born, before my parents were born, you guys hung with what, the Rat Pack and stuff?"

"Sort of. Clara, the important part is that we thought we belonged. We deluded ourselves into thinking we could dabble in human affairs and come out of it unscathed."

Clara reached for the glass he'd just filled. Her mind couldn't wrap around the time-transcending world Santino lived in. "What happened between Vittoria and Howard Hughes?"

"He left her for some actress. She was devastated and tried to kill herself."

"How does one of your kind end their own life?"

"I wish I knew. She only ended up in pain and heartache, but she lived on long after the love of her life passed away in agony. That's our fate, Clara. We watch love die over and over again. Love isn't eternal, but we are."

She finished the glass of wine in silence. It all felt so unfair. "I believe in our happily ever after, Santino. What about with eternals? Can their love not live forever?" Clara asked, desperate for a ray of hope.

Santino set down his glass and looked at her. "As far as our group, as far as I know, there is only one lasting pairing of our kind. Alessandro and Anisa—they worked in our kitchens in Rome. Deeply in love, they were made eternal as part of our household. They are still together. They are the head chefs at Gordon's."

Clara let out a deep breath. "See! Love *can* last, Santino. That is how we will be."

He shook his head. "They are together now, but who knows if they will be in ten years, twenty? What about one hundred years from now, my angel? If, that is, this planet is not destroyed by then."

"Love doesn't die. I refuse to not absorb myself in you out of fear of the end."

Santino collapsed into the leather sofa next to her. "Clara, the thought of watching you die is more than I can bear."

"I'm not asking for that. I'm simply asking for a little time to live before I die. A few more years, maybe? I'm twenty-one; a little more time, that's all."

"And if you get hit by a car tomorrow? Or if you find someone else, a mortal—someone who can give you children, a life? Clara, I'm so ashamed to say that I fear losing you to that—to this life."

"You have to allow me that freedom. Otherwise, our love wasn't real in the first place."

He nodded. "I will honor your wishes, always. But it doesn't hurt any less, my darling."

"I believe," she said, taking his hands in hers, "that our love will be eternal—it will prove you wrong. In five years, maybe ten, we shall be bound together under your blood for eternity. But I can't cross over yet—even though I love you more than I could ever dream."

Thirteen

Back in Vegas, Vittoria faced an angry lover. "How could you do that to her?" She'd just told him about what happened before Clara was attacked—why she happened to be there, in Clara's room that night.

"I know, I told you—I felt horrible. I went to her to tell her that it was staged, that there was nothing like that between Santino and me."

"Well here's the thing V—Clara had guards watching her apartment door when it all went down. I talked to one of them and they sure as hell didn't see you go in." *I've been so blind,* he thought.

"You were so blind, my stud muffin, because you saw in me what you wanted to see. A sexy human woman crazy about you."

"Are you?"

"Sexy?" She shot him a wink.

"Are you crazy about me," he flirted back. As angry as he was, she turned him on faster than anything, even Roswell Aliens.

"We'll talk about the aliens later, they're in the Vatican. And yes, I'm crazy about you."

"Stop reading my mind, it's annoying."

"Fine then. No, Matthew, I'm not human. Not anymore."

He sat down, fearing his knees would buckle if he didn't. "I need a drink," he said as he wiped the sweat from his forehead.

She walked to the mini-bar in the corner of her office and pulled out a Bud Light—a beer she'd stocked just in case he was ever there.

"Stronger. I need bourbon."

She poured the drink and sat across from him. "I can move fast enough to not be seen—my father is the same way. That's why the guards didn't see me that night."

"And when you went in?"

"She was being attacked and I stopped him."

"He was hooded?"

She nodded.

"One of you?"

She nodded again. "I wish Santino were here."

"You don't need him," Matthew said, confidently tossing down his tumbler of bourbon with only a slight cough. "I'm going to figure this out, Vittoria."

"Matthew, no, this is dangerous. This isn't like some blog post where you seek out Elvis sightings—this is deadly."

"He's alive, right? Elvis?"

"Matthew I'm serious."

"Well?"

She nodded with a sigh.

Matthew popped up from the sofa and headed to the bar area. "I knew it!"

After he left, she called Santino in Rome. "I need to put security on Matthew, he's poking around the serial killings too much."

Santino twisted the phone cord around his index finger. "So you want me to protect the man that is *hunting* us?"

"Pretty much," she said. "And you owe it to me. I saved her life, Santino, and you know it."

"Fine," he said with an exhale.

"Oh and one other thing, my prince. He knows what I am now."

"How very observant of him," he joked.

"He thinks he's close to figuring out who the killer is."

There was silence on the line, a click, and then Santino spoke. "He needs to drop it. This line of investigation won't be good for his health."

* * * * *

They'd been in Rome for nearly a week, and Santino wouldn't let Clara out of his sight. She was bored and restless.

"When can we go home? I've already missed a week of classes."

"Did they not transmit your lessons electronically? I spoke to the Dean."

"Oh my God, sometimes you sound eighty. I want to go back. I feel like a caged animal."

"I am simply trying to keep you safe, my angel," Santino said as he turned around in his desk chair. "And I'm far older than eighty."

"I know it's for my own good—but at least let me go out and walk the grounds, I'm going stir-crazy."

"I shall take you out as soon as I finish these emails, I promise." He turned back to his laptop, tapping at the keyboard.

"I'd like to go out alone—unless I'm a prisoner?"

He turned to her. "Of course you are not. You'll stay within the palace walls?"

She smiled and leaned down to kiss him. "I promise. I'm going to walk through that rose garden I can see from our window, and then I'll come back."

Santino loved it when she smiled. "Be back in an hour or I'll send out the hounds," he teased as she left the room.

The weather in Rome was idyllic to Clara. Back home, it was over a hundred degrees every day. Here, it was cool and green—something she wasn't used to. She slipped off her sandals to feel the spongy grass under her toes. Growing up, they'd never had a lawn, always just a water-efficient yard full of rocks. Here, it was like paradise.

The roses were in bloom, and smelled so sweet that she decided to take a few of the crimson ones back to Santino—he loved all things red. She reached down to break one of the stems when she heard it—an animal in pain was wailing from behind the wall of roses.

She pushed the bushes aside, cutting her fingers on the thorns to save the animal, but then she saw them. They did look and sound like animals, in a way, but they were clearly human. Or, they were clearly once human.

On a stone bench, a woman was naked. Her face was pointed toward the sky as she howled, as if summoning the devil in some ancient rite. The woman's long platinum hair was curly, and hung down her back. In front of her crouched a man, stocky with dark body hair, but Clara couldn't see his face. His face was buried in the woman's sex, not in oral sex like Clara knew. This was nothing like the oral pleasure Santino gave her so often—this was brutal, sickening. The man was biting the woman, pulling at her genitals, very literally *eating her.*

Clara was frozen in place—the woman wasn't in pain, she reasoned. But the woman *was* in pain, extreme pain, but she was enjoying it, *getting off on it.* The woman's long red nails clawed into the man's thick head of hair and yanked him up from her—his mouth was covered in blood, his teeth protruding into sharp fangs as he growled at her—like a beast.

As the women's body twisted toward her, she could see the wounds from the man's attack heal as his mouth tore at her nipples, pulling them mercilessly as she clawed at his back until blood flowed from it. "Fuck me, Giovanni," the woman groaned as she slashed at his bloody skin with her sharp nails. He flipped her over, doggy style Clara couldn't help but think, and they did look like dogs mating.

The woman howled as the man thrust into her, his penis swollen and oversized like Clara had never seen before, not even in porn. As the man pumped into the woman, she howled. As he tore open a long gash in her back with his teeth, she screamed again—not like a human, but like a tortured animal.

She turned and ran back to Santino, horrified at what she saw.

"You're bleeding, my angel," he said when she flung open the door to his office.

She was crying too hard to answer him, so he patted his lap for her.

"How did you prick these perfect fingers?" He licked at the droplets of blood dripping from her skin.

"Roses," she managed to say.

"Ah yes, beautiful things can certainly be painful. Why are you so upset?"

She buried her head into his chest. "There were these, these, people and they were clawing each other, howling, it was awful."

"Hm, a fight?"

"Sex. Rough sex. *Really* rough sex."

"A light haired woman with big curls?" He held his hands out to each side of his head.

She nodded. A smile crept across his face. "I fear you've encountered Mother."

Clara shook her head against his chest. "No, she was too young. She couldn't have been older than her forties."

"We started a little earlier with the marriage and the childbearing in the 1500s, my darling. But be careful, she's more than a little off-balance—avoid her if you can."

"I will."

"And Clara, a little exchange of blood is considered pleasurable in my world. You haven't seemed to mind."

"It wasn't a little. It was...barbaric."

"Ah, invoking the poor maligned Barbarians. Anyway, Mother has quite an appetite for men and an even more ravenous lust for blood. She once went around with a bloody shirt just to smell it—I think it was a former lover's."

"Bloody shirt? Did she leave it in your guestroom?"

"I don't know, perhaps. Why?"

"It doesn't matter. I just want to go home."

"Soon, sweet angel, soon."

* * * * *

That evening at sunset, they sat on Santino's balcony, high above the estate. "So you grew up here? This is where you were made eternal?"

He reached for a corkscrew from the iron table and opened the wine.

"I grew up here, but my mother is from Florence."

"And your father?"

"My father was Pope Clement the Seventh." Santino reached for the bottle of Tuscan red and filled their wine glasses.

"Do you mean father in the religious sense? I get that, you were all Catholic back then, right?"

He took a long sip and looked at her. "I mean my biological father was Giulio de' Medici, better known as Pope Clement."

"Oh!"

"You are shocked, my angel?"

"I mean, I knew they weren't exactly celibate. Rodrigo Borgia had an entire family that he acknowledged. And yes, I knew that without watching Showtime," she said with a grin.

Santino laid his hand on her knee. Clara had become his everything in such a short time. "My mother, Octavia de Medici, was the daughter of a prominent cardinal. Her parents were engaged at one time, before he took his vows, so the church considered her legitimate. If you had enough money, enough stature, you did as you pleased."

"Not much has changed in that regard, I suppose," Clara said.

"My mother married a fabulously wealthy banker, Ricardo Marchetti. He loved her, even while she was sleeping with the pope. And, he loved me as his own son, although everyone knew I was Clement's offspring."

"You're hiding me from your mother—is that because she wouldn't approve of you being with a mortal, is that it?"

"Ah," Santino sighed, refilling their glasses. "I don't really care what she approves of. I keep her away from you, and from the family, because she is insane. In eternity, and in her natural life—she's off-balance, dangerous. In the 1940s I had to remove her from power, take control as head of the family. Her madness threatened the living and the eternal."

"Is she still a threat?" Clara's mind drifted to the scene in the garden; she was still shaken by the graphic sex act she'd seen.

"She's always a threat, but I love her. I should have exiled her—there's a place that I cannot speak of where we cast off those of our kind whom we can no longer allow to roam the earth. Instead, I demanded she stay here and never leave. But, she disobeys. Last month she showed up at the Roman, other times she's made herself at home in my penthouse. She's hard to control."

"There are others, though? Cast off from the...is it a coven, what?"

"I supposed you could use that word, some do. I prefer family. And yes, there are other exiles. Not many, nine now."

"How did it happen? I mean, you were a man living in Rome once, right? Were you married to Vittoria when you were taken?"

A dark veil swept across Santino's face. Those months before it happened weren't things he wanted to remember, and yet, every time he closed his eyes he saw them—starved and desperate. Most of the children died horrific deaths before the cardinal came.

"You don't have to talk about it," Clara said, running her fingers across his forearm to calm him.

"I want to. As far as Vittoria, our marriage was annulled after a year. We weren't compatible in that way—it wasn't hard to convince Father to annul it himself. Her father, however, never forgave me. He saw it as a dishonor to his family, to their name, and has always hated me."

"He's alive? I mean, he's a vamp-I mean an eternal?"

Santino nodded. "Yes, he's been exiled. By me, unfortunately."

Clara leaned back in her chair. There was so much she didn't understand.

He began to speak again. "It was 1527, and Rome was under siege. My entire household retreated to the Castel Sant'Angelo with the pope to seek refuge from the invaders. We were held hostage for weeks—they surrounded us. That's when *he* came."

"He?"

"Grandfather. The cardinal—many said he had the devil inside him, that he'd taken some dark oath. He only appeared at night. The pope brought me into his chambers with Mother and the cardinal late one night in early June, well into the siege. 'Tonight my son you will die so that you will live forever,' my father said."

"But the pope didn't, I mean I know that Clement continued on long after, surely he wasn't an eternal?"

"No, the pope didn't partake in the solution offered by the cardinal. But I did, as did Mother and all of our household, many nobles, such as Nicco's father, Vittoria's family, and all of our servants. Reginald, who pretended to be a waiter and slipped you the drug that day, he was our gamekeeper."

Clara's jaw fell open. "So, that night one man made over a hundred vampires? He is *that* strong?"

"No, angel, that night he made only us—Mother and me. The next night, we continued to save the others, and it continued down from there. That is why we are the strongest—mother and I are made directly from the cardinal. But there are other factors that have a role in strength, of course, but our source blood is the purest of our family."

"And your father? I mean, Octavia's husband, Marchetti?"

Santino's face fell into his hands. "He wouldn't join us," Santino finally said, his grieved voice barely above a whisper. "We begged him, pleaded—but he called it evil, he refused. Clara, he was a good man, not evil like us."

"You were and are a good man!" Her heart ached for him, for the pain he'd lived through.

"I didn't see him after that first night. I believe he died during the horror that followed—the Sack of Rome."

"And the cardinal? Your grandfather? Is he still a part of your family?"

Santino shook his head. "I've never seen him again, either, after that first night when he fed us his blood."

Fourteen

"He has to go back, Mother," Santino said as he stood on the long terrace that spanned the length of the palace and overlooked the gardens.

"I know," Octavia said.

"It was bad enough when I allowed you to stay in Rome, but Giovanni Farnese? If word gets out that he is roaming free, I'll have a civil war on my hands."

"He was once your father-in-law." She walked over and stood next to Santino, resting her hands on the polished railing.

"And he's hated me ever since. Mother, how could you do this to me?"

"To you," she shouted, turning to face him. "To *you*. You are such a selfish, ungrateful tyrant."

Santino said nothing, but in a rare daytime gesture, he pulled a cigarette from his pocket and lit it.

Octavia reached for one, and he lit hers as it dangled from her lips.

"I've been lonely, my prince. Giovanni is the only man I've been with since you ousted me."

"You've been with scores of men," Santino said with an exhale of smoke.

"Mortals, they are like pets, I mean real men."

He shook his head. "Before we were made eternal, you would have nothing to do with Farnese."

"Well, he's hairy," she laughed. "And short, but he has been all I've had since the second human war."

"And his current thoughts on me?"

Octavia put her hand on his forearm. "He will respect you as my son. But, of course, he still believes that I am queen and should rule as such."

"What do you think, Octavia?"

She leaned back, the breeze blowing her curly mane of hair behind her. "I believe that you are meant to lead this family. You are a Medici, the son of a pope, through you flows the blood of kings, and despite not listening to your mother, I am content with the current state of things."

They were silent until the sound of a helicopter distracted them. Octavia cocked her head into the breeze, listening.

"And this human?" Octavia said when the helicopter noise stopped.

"I need Clara, Mother. Not like a pet and not like a diversion."

"Then like what?"

"Like for eternity."

He snuffed out the half-smoked cigarette and turned toward the door. To his back she said, "Oh, my child, you are in for a world of pain. Also, Vittoria just arrived in that chopper—with yet another mortal. It's raining humans."

* * * * *

"Why did you bring him here?" Santino paced the marble floor in front of Vittoria.

"You shouldn't smoke."

"You know it doesn't matter." She was trying to diffuse him.

"It smells bad. What does Clara think about—"

"Cut the bullshit, Vittoria. Why is he here?"

"Matthew *knows* who the killer is—he's figured out the mystery, and that puts him in danger in Las Vegas. I brought him here for the same reason as you did Clara—to keep him safe."

Santino stopped pacing and ran his hands through his hair. "What is it with you and this nosy mortal? You do know he wants to kill our kind? Does he yet know that *you* are part of the vermin he wants to eradicate?"

She relaxed a little, sensing that she would get her way, at least for a while. Other than Nicco, she'd been the closest to Santino since he'd made her eternal on that dark night in Rome so long ago. "He knows, yes."

With a sigh, he asked, "Who then does the brilliant Hunter think is the killer?"

"Well," Vittoria said, bracing for the sure return of Santino's anger. "He won't say. He wants an interview, with you, for his book, and after that he will tell you and help in any way that he can. Matthew won't betray us."

Santino couldn't help but chuckle at the absurdity of it all. "*Interview with a Vampire*, he knows it's been done?"

"Please, *mio principe*, for me—I love him. I've never asked anything of you, not even for my father to be spared, but this—let me spend what little time I can with this blond curiosity. He makes me happy for the first time in...eternity."

Santino reached for her—she and Nicco, and now Clara, were the only true friends he had, the only ones he'd allowed into his troubled soul. "I'll talk to him tomorrow, he has an hour. The Hunter can stay but you watch him closely—if he wanders, starts to snoop, he goes home. And for the love of God keep him away from Octavia."

She turned to leave; she wanted to get back to Matthew. He'd confided in her that he had an odd sense of being followed by a dark presence, and it worried her.

She froze as Santino spoke again. "Vittoria, one other thing. Giovanni was here earlier. He's gone now."

A shiver ran through her as she turned to look at Santino. "Why is Father walking free?"

"Octavia," was his only explanation.

Matthew was busy looking through her room when she returned. "Is he pissed?"

"Not nearly as much as I thought he'd be. He's fairly preoccupied—you are the least of his worries right now."

"Thank you for bringing me here. I won't take advantage of your trust, I promise. I'll behave."

"You'd better, my Hunter, because we've been known to put troublemakers up on spikes around here."

* * * * *

"You have a phone call," Vittoria said when Santino opened the door to his suite of rooms the next morning.

"Who is it?" he asked, glancing at his own phone screen to see if the caller had tried him there first.

"The *other* prince," she answered with a toothy grin.

"Shit, what does he want?"

"I don't know, he wouldn't say." She turned to leave, her heels clicking along the marble floor as Santino followed her to the rooms they'd set up as an office in his family's palace.

"What do you want, Franco?" Santino asked his older brother.

"News of these *vampire* murders is all over New Orleans—and you're sitting in Rome with your mortal lover? What the fuck, man?"

"And you sit doing nothing but smoking weed with witches in New Orleans, my brother. If you have a problem with it, head to the Roman and help me out."

Franco was silent for a moment before saying, "I don't do Vegas, you know that. Besides, I wasn't the son of the pope, now was I? I'm just a Marchetti, after all. But seriously, dude, do you know who this asswipe is?"

Santino bit into the side of his cheek—his half brother had embraced eternal living by trying to always be current, which caused him to follow trends, and usually it made him sound two steps behind. "I am not sure, but I have a lead. I might know something later this morning."

"Cool," Franco said. "Jennifer is totally freaked the fuck out about it."

"What does your witch care about the dealing of eternals in Las Vegas?"

Franco took a deep breath. He knew Santino loathed the fact that he was sleeping with a witch. "She doesn't, but Estrella in San Francisco said that you brought it there, they are convinced you are the one preying on humans."

"And why would I do that?" *Fucking busybody witches,* Santino thought.

"Hey man, you wouldn't. But someone has it in for you. Let me ask you this—where was Octavia when all this went down?"

"Mother may be mental, but she wouldn't hurt me."

"No, you're her golden boy," Franco snapped.

"I broke her heart and you know it. Shit, Franco, I hope you're not right."

"Me too, man, me too. I've gotta go, drop a dime on me later." Santino cringed as his brother hung up. *Why did he have to talk like that?*

* * * * *

"You have a brother?" Clara stared at Santino incredulously as he closed the door behind him.

"Indeed," Santino said, walking over to pour coffee from the silver urn on the side table.

"What's he like?" She couldn't imagine a sibling of Santino.

"He's hairy."

Clara reached for the china mug of coffee Santino handed her. "Hairy like a werewolf?"

"For the hundredth time, darling, there are no werewolves. But no, hairy like a hipster, I suppose. Bearded, and luckily for him it's en vogue again. He hates to not be trendy."

"Oh, so just like you," she teased the old-fashioned Santino.

Santino leaned over to kiss her. Clara was the only person who teased him. "I adore you, you know. Let's go back to bed," he said, running his finger across her bare shoulder.

"You said you'd meet with Matthew this morning."

"Ah, yes, the oh-so-original interview."

"Do you think he knows who the killer is? I like Matthew, but I think he's just using that as a carrot to dangle to spend some time with you. He's a little like a fanboy," she said with a wink.

"Matthew Hunter is smart and resourceful—I won't discount his thoughts on the matter." Santino glanced at his watch. "We have twenty minutes, plenty of time to revisit the sheets?'

She pushed his wandering fingers away from her thigh. "Not the way you do things, my love. You'd barely be finished with my toes in twenty minutes."

"I do love those toes... Okay, I'll be back. Please stay here until I return? My brother Franco had some rather disturbing ideas regarding the state of things."

* * * * *

Matthew paced back and forth along the wide terrace at the rear of the palace. He'd thrown up three times that morning—he was going to finally get into Santino's mind. The leader of the most powerful family of eternals on earth was going to talk exclusively to him, and Matthew knew it would be life changing. And on top of it, thanks to some help from his vast network of contacts, along with his father's research on Santino's coven, he knew who was plaguing the streets of Las Vegas. He just didn't really know why.

"Tell me the story of your origination," he said aloud, rehearsing. "No, that sounds stupid. I need to keep it conversational." He turned to walk the length of the terrace again, and as he did, the killer struck.

The attacker flew into him with enough force to fling Matthew to the ground, his skull smashing to the tile below with a sickening crack. The monster wore no hood this time—this kill wasn't planned like the others. It was pure impulse. He'd heard that this Hunter intended to reveal his identity to the prince—and he couldn't have that. Giovanni couldn't risk losing Octavia, not yet.

In a ferocious squeeze, he cracked the feeble human's ribs as if they were made of Styrofoam, and baring his teeth, he sank them into the fat artery in Matthew's neck—sucking fast and hard, not for pleasure, but to finish the Hunter as quickly as possible. His nimble fingers tore open the human's chest as he devoured him like a Velociraptor in a horror movie.

Giovanni was so intent on getting rid of this nosy human that he didn't sense the other immortal behind them, and by the time Santino tore open the monster's back, it was too late. Santino was too strong, and within seconds Giovanni, blood pouring from his mouth, human tissue hanging from his hands, was dead. Santino drained the monster of his blood, struggling to consume it all. Sick from the bitter evil that was Giovanni's blood, Santino curled up into a ball.

Clara came running when she heard Vittoria scream from the arched doorway to the terrace—a scream so pathetic, so desperate, it caused bumps up her spine. Vittoria was howling, "Matthew! No! Who did this?"

"Your father, dear," Octavia said from behind them. She walked across the tiles and looked at

Santino, prostrate on the ground, violently ill from the blood ingestion.

"Vittoria, do it," Santino said, pointing toward the Hunter's mangled corpse. "Take him, you have my permission."

Vittoria ran toward Matthew. "Santino, please, he's too mauled. I'm not strong enough, help me!"

She ripped open her arm with her sharp teeth and began to drip her own blood into Matthew's mouth. "It's too bad, he's too far gone," she wailed.

"Mother, please, for me," Santino's raspy voice begged from the ground. He was far too weak to even move—there was no way he could give eternal blood to the Hunter.

Octavia looked to her dead lover, then to her son and nodded. "For you, Santino."

Her blood was strong, and as she fed this former enemy, she knew he would survive. When it was done, when his newly-pale eyes fluttered open, Octavia looked to the young human who was now cradling Santino's head. Clara was green, sick from what she'd seen.

"So this is the waif that has stolen your heart?" she snapped at Santino as he clung to Clara.

"Let it be, Mother."

"Well," Octavia said with the wave of her hand, "she seems to be the only human left. Welcome to the fold, Hunter." She frowned at him—she'd have never given her blood to this hater of her kind if Santino hadn't pleaded with her to do so.

"Shed a few tears for your father, Vittoria, before we burn his corpse. I know I will—well, maybe. He was a demon, sure, but a great fuck."

Vittoria gasped as Santino's eyes met his mother's. "Go, now."

"Yes, my prince," she said as she walked into the house, her flowing white dress billowing behind her.

Clara stared at Matthew as he sat up. His eyes glowed—the deep blue had been transformed into the paleness of the other eternals' eyes. "I don't feel any different," he said incredulously. "A little achy, but I still feel like me," he said, staring at his hands.

"You are you, Hunter, just you—forever," Santino said.

"But Giovanni wasn't forever—it is possible to die."

"True," Santino conceded. "A much stronger being can take the life of another. Witches can be particularly dangerous."

"Witches exist?" Matthew couldn't wrap his mind around any of it.

"Indeed. But the scariest beings are the werewolves. They'll suck your brains out through your ear." Santino pointed to his head.

"I knew it!" Matthew said. "I knew werewolves were real. I saw one once on the Strip."

Santino chuckled. "I'm messing with you, as Clara would say. There is no such thing as werewolves—it's just a myth."

"Ah," Matthew said, relaxing. "And I knew there weren't really witches."

"Oh witches are very real, and do not approve of our kind, my love," Vittoria said.

"I'm sorry about your father," Clara said to Vittoria. "I know he did bad things, but still."

"He strangled my mother in her sleep when I was a child. She's smiling from somewhere today." She reached a hand to Matthew. "We have quite a journey ahead."

* * * * *

The next morning, before their private jet took them back to Vegas, the Hunter got his interview with the prince of the vampires, Santino the Eternal. The blog he decided to abandon, but he was determined to publish his book. He changed the names, and any details that would cause too much scrutiny, but he knew he had a bestseller on his hands.

"Can I ask you one last question, off the record," Matthew said, closing his notebook.

"You can ask," Santino answered.

"I zeroed in on the serial killer by looking at my father's records of the family through the ages. There were a handful of eternals who disappeared from history, and only one of them fit the description of the man who placed the body under the bridge in San Francisco."

"Did you know he was Vittoria's father?"

Matthew shook his head. "No, the modernizing of the names threw me."

"What's your question?"

"Why was he exiled?"

Santino's lips curled up in a rare smile. "When we were in London, he was cutting open prostitutes."

"Wait? He was Jack the Ripper?"

Santino nodded. "I would have killed him then if it weren't for Vittoria."

Fifteen

"It's so hot," Clara moaned, dipping her toe into the tiny plunge pool on Santino's terrace.

"It always feels worse here around all this concrete. Come out to the 'burbs this afternoon," Nicco said as he sipped a Corona.

"Nicco, I don't have time to spend an afternoon out in Henderson. I have work to do."

"You always have work to do," Clara whined. "Please? One afternoon. I've never seen Nicco's house."

Santino looked over at Clara and smiled. She'd changed his life, this young human, and he knew he would never be the same again. And he didn't want to be. Life before Clara was dark, and now, her lightness shone all around him.

"I suppose I could work poolside?"

"Sure boss," Nicco answered. "Lightning fast Wi-Fi."

"Let me change and I suppose we shall make the four hour drive to the edge of the earth so that we can see grass," Santino teased as he pulled off his tie.

In the light traffic of mid-day, it only took twenty-five minutes to reach Nicco's sprawling suburban house, and within an hour the three of them sat beside his pool. "Where's Rachel?" Clara asked. Nicco had fallen for a human himself over the course of the summer, and she and Clara had become friends.

"She took Sunny to the new aquarium—you know that one they just built in the mall? It's supposed to be hands on."

"Oh yeah, I might make Mr. Recluse take me there." She reached for another bottle of beer from the cooler. "Hey do you have any more limes?"

"Probably," Nicco answered. "Let me ask Hilda—she's in the kitchen starting dinner."

Clara stood up and let her towel fall from her. As Santino watched, she dove into the water and gracefully spanned the length of the pool. He toyed with the idea of joining her when he heard Nicco yell for him.

In the kitchen, Santino took a deep breath when he saw it—a woman was hanging from Nicco's light fixture, her white sensible shoes hovering several inches from his granite island.

"I assume this is Hilda?" Santino said. He held his hand up to Clara through the open door as she walked toward the kitchen. "One minute, darling," he said, pointing toward a chaise lounge by the side of the pool. Clara could not see this mess.

"Y-yes," Nicco said with a hard swallow. "Why would anyone do this? We were feet away! I heard her come in not more than twenty minutes ago."

"Nicco, she is not yet gone. Talk to her."

Nicco snapped his head toward Santino. "I will not! Her soul deserves respect."

"This," Santino said, pointing toward the hanging body of Nicco's housekeeper, "is not a crime committed by a mortal. Her head is twisted completely around and there are markings on her flesh. We need to know what evil came into your house and desecrated your domestic staff."

"She was Hilda, she's been with me for five years, she's not——"

"Fine. Find out what happened to your Hilda."

Nicco took a deep breath and looked at the hanging woman. He could hear her as her soul left her body.

"I know, ma'am, I know. The pain will stop very soon—you will cross over into a better place," Nicco told her.

Santino rolled his eyes at the lie, but nodded to Nicco to continue.

"Her neck hurts," Nicco said, "but she said a black haired woman appeared from nowhere, just formed from the air, and broke her neck." Nicco shot Santino a knowing look. "The dark haired woman had a long scar across her cheek and eyes of gold."

"Deborah," Santino said with the shake of his head. "Let her pass through, Nicco. Relieve her pain and clean up. I need to pacify Clara."

Santino walked back to join Clara poolside. "We cannot find any limes, my angel," he said as if nothing were amiss.

"Limes? Oh yeah, never mind that, what's wrong in there? I heard Nicco scream and then you ran in there. What's going on, Santino?"

Santino laid his hand on top of hers. "Oh, that," he said. "It seems his housekeeper has been taken in some ancient ritual of witchcraft by my sister. I believe it's under control for the time being, but we may just have another adventure in our near future."

She stared at him incredulously as he reached for a bottle of beer and popped the cap off with a quick electrical spark from his index finger.

He clinked the bottle against hers and said, "Cheers, my darling Clara. I love you, for eternity."

THE END

The Author and the Muse

An Eternal Series Short

"Stop haunting me, Santino." My nails stopped their staccato tapping on the worn MacBook keys as I peered at the elegant man who'd just materialized in my kitchen.

"*Haunting,* that's funny, Samantha," he answered as his palms straightened the lapels of his tailored suit.

"Is that Armani?"

"Is that Banana Republic?" he shot back with a wink.

"Outlet," I admitted, pouring another glass of cabernet. After a long sip I asked, "What do you want with me? I don't write P-R-N or whatever. It's not my genre, I'm not the author for you."

He reached for the bottle and read the label. "Ah, the good stuff. May I?"

"No, you may not. It's wasted on you—you don't even feel it." I took the bottle from him, topping off my glass with the scrunch of my nose, a bad habit of mine.

"I enjoy the taste, if you must know, even though my body doesn't register the effect of such things."

"Does wine give you that same sensation as drinking blood?" I asked, unable to quell my curiosity about my strange new companion.

He glanced longingly once more at the deep red wine in my glass before he answered with a sigh, "No, Sam, it doesn't, and I've haven't drank blood in many years."

I raised an eyebrow in disbelief. As a writer, I usually sensed when a character was lying.

"Okay, not in a *couple* of years, then, and it was only recreationally. And he *wanted* it. Can we get back to Clara? I want her to live forever."

"You know that can never happen, Santino."

"I know, I know, but through your book our story, our love, will live forever—even if she cannot."

"I get that. There are several talented P-R-whatever writers out there. Get one of them to—"

"It's called P-N-R, paranormal romance, but this isn't *about* genre. It's about *us*, our story, Clara and me. What happened to love is love, no boundaries, all of that?"

"Now you're using my own words against me." I took a deep breath as the thrill of a new tale sparked a fire to write deep within me.

"Why me, Santino? I'm in the middle of this pirate novella right now. I can't." I shook my head and glanced at my laptop screen again.

"I don't know why, but *you* must write it. Our story isn't about *what I am*, it's about love, the same as your other books. *Please?*"

"Okay, okay," I acquiesced. "I'll see where your love leads, after *Deeper*."

He smiled at me for the first time. Santino's ageless pale blue eyes glistened with a preternatural glow as he pulled out a pack of cigarettes from his inside jacket pocket. "Let's smoke in celebration."

I groaned at him, shooing him back into the background with the wave of my hand. "You know I'm not supposed to."

"Humans and their silly lungs," he said with a chuckle as he faded back to that special place between reality and the lunatic dreams of a writer.

I turned my attention once again to Sir James Morgan and his virgin captive, Lucinda, as the faint scent of his Marlboro lingered in the dry air.

ACKNOWLEDGEMENTS

As always, I'd like to that my patient family for allowing me to give birth to Santino and Clara—I loved every second of writing this book. To my tireless assistant, Kelly Mallett—I couldn't have done it without you. To my reader group, Hunt's Hideaway, you make me smile every day. To the volunteers who work their backsides off for me, Hunt's Hustlers: Melissa Aguirre, Ashley Carr, Jessica Cecconi, Reva Coomer, Tina England, Laura Frasher, Missy Harton, Mindy Knadler, Kelly Mallett, Ann Myers, and Jenny Shepherd. Thank you to the review team who read this book early, gave me feedback, and cheered me on during those final few weeks: Alison, AnnaMarie, Emma Jane Marie, Janine, Jen, Kathleen, Melissa, Missy, Ratula, Tara, Theresa M, Theresa T, and Tina.

Also to my editors, Missy Borucki and Kelly Mallett—thank you for polishing the words. To my all-important proofreaders, Carol Hall and Daphne Caldwell—thank you yet again.
Eric Battershell, Clarise Tan, and Johnny Kane—thank you for a stunning cover to wrap around the words. I value the blogs and event promoters that continue to support indie romance, and am forever grateful. But

most of all thank you, dear reader, for taking a chance
on my first paranormal romance.

--Sam, March 21st, 2017.

ABOUT THE AUTHOR

Sam JD Hunt resides in Las Vegas with her husband, the inspiration for the young Thomas Hunt character, as well as her two children.

When not writing, Hunt enjoys travel, community involvement, spending time with friends and family, and hiking. She spends her days writing and trying to answer the age-old question: is it too late for coffee or too early for wine?

Word-of-mouth is crucial for any author to succeed. If you enjoyed this book, please leave a review on Amazon. Even if it were just a sentence or two, it would make all the difference and would be very much appreciated.